THE
SCIENCE OF
BREAKABLE
THINGS

THE
SCIENCE OF
BREAKABLE
THINGS

TAE KELLER

Random House New York

Text copyright © 2018 by Tae Keller
Jacket art and interior illustrations copyright © 2018 by Alexandria Neonakis

All rights reserved. Published in the United States by Random House Children's Books, a division of Penguin Random House LLC, New York.

Random House and the colophon are registered trademarks of Penguin Random House LLC.

Visit us on the Web! rhcbooks.com

Educators and librarians, for a variety of teaching tools, visit us at RHTeachersLibrarians.com

Library of Congress Cataloging-in-Publication Data
Names: Keller, Tae, author.
Title: The science of breakable things / Tae Keller.
Description: First edition. | New York : Random House, [2018] | Summary: Middle schooler Natalie's yearlong assignment to answer a question using the scientific process leads to truths about her mother's depression and her own cultural identity.
Identifiers: LCCN 2016057633 | ISBN 978-1-5247-1566-3 (hardcover) | ISBN 978-1-5247-1568-7 (ebook) | ISBN 978-1-5247-1567-0 (lib. bdg.)
Subjects: | CYAC: Middle schools—Fiction. | Schools—Fiction. | Friendship—Fiction. | Family problems—Fiction. | Science—Methodology—Fiction. | Depression, Mental—Fiction. | Racially mixed people—Fiction.
Classification: LCC PZ7.1.K418 ScI 2018 | DDC [Fic]—dc23

Printed in the United States of America
10 9 8 7 6 5 4 3 2 1
First Edition

Random House Children's Books supports the First Amendment and celebrates the right to read.

STEP 1: OBSERVE

This is the first step in the scientific process! Sharpen and hone your observational skillz! What is going on in the world around you? Note everything you see and experience!

#MrNeelysScientificAdventure

ASSIGNMENT 1: OBSERVE YOUR SURROUNDINGS

Mr. Neely just wrote our first lab book assignment on the board in his scrunched-up, scratchy handwriting, and he's getting all excited about this scientific process stuff. I'm not sure why he feels the need to use hashtags and spell perfectly innocent words with a *z*, but he's one of those teachers you don't bother questioning.

He has big plans for this lab notebook. Apparently, he thinks it's important to teach students "dedication to long-term projects," and this assignment is his grand solution. Basically, we're supposed to observe something that interests us and spend all year applying the scientific process to our capital-*Q* Question.

As soon as we sat down, he passed out these dorky old composition notebooks and said, "This will be your Wonderings journal! You will record lab notes and assignments, and document the greatest scientific journey of all time—*your* scientific journey!"

We all stared, trying to figure out if he was for real or not. He was.

"You'll spend this year developing your own scientific process, and it all starts with one question—that thing that sparks you to life." Mr. Neely made a weird explosion gesture with his hands, and someone in the back of the room giggled, which only seemed to encourage him. "By the end of the year, *I'll* be the one learning. From *you*!"

Mr. Neely is a new teacher, so he's still all optimistic and stuff, but personally I think this assignment's a lost cause. Last year, our English teacher, Mrs. Jackson, thought it'd be really great for us to keep journals. The only requirement: fifty pages by the end of the year, written from the heart. If you haven't guessed already, that just resulted in everyone writing all fifty pages the day before the journals were due. I mostly filled mine with song lyrics, copied in my biggest, sloppiest handwriting.

And technically, this is supposed to be homework, but I don't see why I shouldn't get a head start. Without further ado, dearest lab notebook, I present Natalie Napoli's Scientific Observations:[1]

- Mr. Neely waves his arms in big circles when he talks, which makes him look like an overeager hula dancer. His white button-down—bright against his dark brown skin—wrinkles as he moves.
- He tells us he wants us to "embrace the joys of science."
- Mikayla Menzer raises her hand.
- Mikayla Menzer answers without being called on. She says, "Science is literally the joy of my life. I am literally embracing it right now."
- Mikayla Menzer is not literally embracing anything. She's just sitting at her desk, catty-corner to mine, with her hands clasped in front of her, and her thick dark braid twisting over her shoulder.
- Mikayla Menzer smells like sunscreen, which kind of makes the entire classroom smell like sunscreen, and the air in here is damp and hot. I wish Fountain Middle had air-conditioning.

---

[1] Only the most brilliant observations you'll ever read. Imagine you're hearing a drumroll right now. Go on, imagine it.

- I wish we had enough money for me to go to Valley Hope Middle, which does have AC, but now that Mom's "sick," Dad says we need to "tighten our belt a notch."
- And anyway, Twig's here, even though her family can definitely afford Valley Hope, so I guess this place isn't so bad.[2]
- Mr. Neely is saying my name, but I haven't been listening, so I just nod at him and give him my best *I'm embracing science* smile.
- Mr. Neely says, "I'm glad you're having so much fun with the assignment, but making observations is supposed to be homework, Natalie. Please pay attention in class."
- I am paying attention.
- And Mikayla Menzer still smells like sunscreen.

---

[2] Twig: best friend in the entire galaxy. (Her words.)

STEP 2: QUESTION

What baffles you about the world? Find something that intrigues you and study it with all your heart! Don your detective cap and become your own private investigator! Or, should I say, your own *scientific* investigator!

#SeventhGradeSleuths

ASSIGNMENT 2: QUESTIONING

Mr. Neely had us go around and read our scientific questions out loud today. So Tom K. said, "What's the maximum voltage before a battery implodes?" and Mikayla Menzer said, "How will plants grow if raised in different light conditions?"[3]

I hadn't done the homework, and by the time he got to me, I still hadn't thought of a question, so I blurted, "Why does Mr. Neely use so many hashtags?"

My cheeks got hot right away and my palms started to itch, because I'd never insulted a teacher like that. But

---

[3] Mikayla Menzer, *n.:* Cheaty McCheater, because I know for a fact she's done that experiment before.

Twig busted out laughing and gave me a thumbs-up from across the room. Mikayla rolled her eyes and flipped her braid from one shoulder to the other.[4]

Nobody else knew how to react, and they basically looked at each other like, *Is she serious or joking?!*

Mr. Neely smiled, because for all that energy of his, apparently he's pretty patient. I felt the knots in my stomach untangle. "That question doesn't *quite* prompt scientific investigation! Keep searching the world around you for a valid question!"

To be honest, it was kind of embarrassing, because I hadn't expected everyone else to take the assignment seriously, and it didn't help that Dari, new-kid-slash-class-genius, read his question right after mine and said some annoyingly smart stuff about acute angles or whatever. So now I have to come up with a new question, and I'm not sure what to ask.

In other news, Mom didn't come out of her room for dinner again, which was extra bad tonight because Dad went to all this trouble making it. When I came home from school, he was hovering over some fat, old cookbook, trying to stuff herbs into a chicken, and the water in a pot of pasta started bubbling over the edge.

I stood there staring, not sure whether this was funny

---

4   Mikayla's obsessed with braids and knows how to do all different styles. I used to let her braid my hair, but not anymore.

or sad, until Dad yelped, "Natalie, stop standing there and help me!"

So that was what Dad and I did for the next hour, him cooking and me measuring ingredients, and it was nice. We didn't even need to talk. Dad's a therapist, so whenever we do talk, he asks me a bunch of questions and says things like, "And how are you feeling?" To which I always answer, "Annoyed."

Anyway, the whole kitchen smelled wonderful, and the chicken tasted surprisingly good. But when Dad and I set the table for dinner, Mom didn't even come out of their bedroom.

"Should I go get her?" I asked.

Dad gave me this sad smile and said, "I think she needs space right now," which seemed to be his answer for everything Mom-related these days.

"But don't you think she should be here?"

"I would like that, but we need to give your mother some space."

"But, Dad."

"But, Natalie."

We ate the rest of the dinner in silence, only this time it was the bad kind of silence, and the food stopped tasting so good.

Later, I tried to think of a scientific question for Mr. Neely, but I just kept thinking, over and over, like an annoying song stuck in my head, *Mom would've helped me with this.*

Whenever I'd had science or math questions for school in the past, we'd sit down at the dining table and spread all my worksheets and equations and diagrams out in front of us. She'd twist up her strawberry-blond hair and clip it back, because for Mom that meant Business, and we'd get to work.

She'd think of an experiment for everything and anything. *You don't get chemical reactions? We'll inflate a balloon using baking soda and vinegar! Can't figure out water density? No problem, let's build a lava lamp!*

It didn't matter that I was bad at science, not when I had Mom to help me. Our kitchen would end up looking like a war zone, and Dad would walk in and act all mad like, *I won't be cleaning up this time!* Even though we knew he would.

He always did.

But now Mom's in the bedroom and Dad's cleaning the kitchen, and it won't take him long. I think even he misses her mess.

Now I'm sitting alone, realizing I can't think of the experiment that will explain everything. How can I get the answer when I don't even know the question?

ASSIGNMENT 3: FROGS!

Mr. Neely sprang a doozy on us today.

"Guess what, class!" His eyes were big behind his black-framed glasses, and his bald head glinted under the fluorescent classroom lights.

Nobody responded.

"Guess what," he repeated, only this time he didn't wait for a response. "We're doing dissections today! Hashtag: frog dissections."

Everybody started whispering at once. This was only our second week of school, and most teachers don't hand knives out before they've even learned their students' last names—even if they're only tiny frog-cutting knives.[5]

---

5   Scalpels, for the record.

But Mr. Neely grinned and passed out a list of safety instructions. "We've been lucky enough to receive an *unexpected opportunity,* and like true scientific explorers, we will make the best of it!" he said—which, knowing Fountain Middle, was probably code for: the school messed up and ordered a whole bunch of dead frogs way too early.

Mr. Neely kept talking. "We're going to open up these frogs and see what makes them tick. You never truly know how an organism works until you see what's going on inside."

We all kind of grimaced, because, gross.

Mikayla raised her hand and spoke before being called on, again. "Mr. Neely, you know how much I love science, but I literally can't do it. It's against human rights."

Mr. Neely frowned. "Well, I suppose I can't force you, Mikayla, if you feel this is against *animal* rights. You can sit in the hallway by the lockers and fill out a worksheet."

Janie, Mikayla's best friend, raised her hand and explained that she, too, believed in animal rights and must be removed from the experiment.

Mr. Neely sighed. "Anybody else?"

Personally, I'm more comfortable with plants than dead animals. But considering the choice had become dissecting a frog or hanging out with Mikayla and Janie, I chose the less vile option.

It's not like I hate Mikayla. Not really. It's more that there's this black cloud of awkward whenever we're together, and everything feels all wrong. Sometimes I don't know where the old Mikayla went—the one who made magic potions with me while our moms worked together, the one who dug up dirt and helped me pack it into test tubes. I used to think someone else replaced her overnight with a Not-Mikayla who was not-my-best-friend, but now I try not to think about her at all.

Mr. Neely sped through a two-minute lesson on what we were actually supposed to be learning from this whole dissection business, but none of us were listening. We were too busy scanning the room and silently making important partner arrangements for our first lab of the school year.

Twig and I looked at each other immediately. She didn't actually need to ask, since of course we were going to work together, but she made an exaggerated *you, me?* gesture, and I grinned and nodded back.

As soon as Mr. Neely finished explaining safety precautions, we both hurried over to claim the lab table in the far back. It's in a corner that Mr. Neely can't really see, so it's obviously the best. Twig was moving at double speed, and by the time I pulled out my notebook, she'd already organized our materials. Our materials being, you know, the dead frog and such.

She tied her blond hair back haphazardly, so random strands hung loose from the ponytail. "I'm so excited about this, Natalie. Can you believe it? Can I cut first? I wanna see the heart. And maybe the bladder. Frog pee: gross or cool?" Twig was talking fast in her usual way, excited about things nobody should be excited about.

"You can cut the whole time," I said, as if I were making a grand sacrifice.

Twig squealed. "It'll be like Operation!"

That's the thing about Twig: she's obsessed with games. Not video games like most people, but those old board games nobody actually likes to play. Although, to be fair, she makes me play those games a lot, and I actually do enjoy them. Twig has a way of making things fun.

And I hate to admit it, but I started getting into the dissection, too. I wasn't cutting the frog open or anything, but I started narrating as Twig sliced, like Twig was one of those doctors on TV. I even made the little heart-monitor beeping sound.

Then Twig leaned in close to the frog's stomach and shouted, "Holy cow! Holy cow!" I looked over her shoulder to see she'd cut open the stomach and found a grasshopper in there, totally intact. Stomach grasshoppers: decidedly cool.

Mr. Neely came over to see what was going on, and

he got excited, too. "Class, look at what these scientific explorers found!" he said.

And then the whole class was crowding around us and saying, "So cool" and "Oh, gross." Even Genius Dari came over to look, and I could tell he was upset that his frog hadn't had a nice dinner before dying.

Dari bent over our lab table for a better look at the frog. His arms were stiff at his sides as he fidgeted with the bottom of his T-shirt. Finally, he gave us a reluctant "Well done" before walking back to his own table.

Twig stuck her tongue out at him behind his back. Only it's too bad because Mr. Neely noticed, and we were no longer his star pupils.

MATERIALS:
- 1 scalpel, sharp
- 1 pair of tweezers, metal
- 2 pairs of gloves, rubber
- 1 frog, dead

PROCEDURE:
1. Let Twig do the dirty work.
2. Let Twig discover dead grasshopper.
3. Collect bragging rights.

• • •

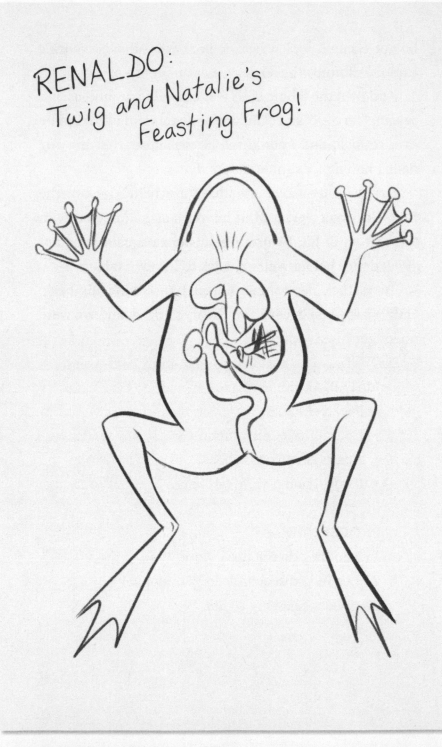

After school, Twig invited me back to her house, which we figured we could get away with under the pretense of doing our frog lab reports.

I dialed Dad, and Twig leaned over. "Tell Yeong-jin I say hello!" she shouted into my ear and the receiver.[6] I waved her off.

Dad sounded tired when he answered, and when I asked to go to Twig's, he got all concerned-sounding. Hanging out with Twig after school had never been a problem before, but since this summer, things have been different. "Natalie, I think it would be best if you came right home. I don't want you running away from this situation."

Dad's always calling Mom a "situation" and making a bigger deal about things than they need to be. He thinks the "situation" is really bothering me, and it is, I guess, but it's not like she's really sick, even though that's how Dad keeps referring to her. The way I see it, she just got bored with life—bored with us. I'm not going to waste my time being sad about it.

"It's not like I'm sneaking out in the middle of the night and running away from home. I just want to go to Twig's for a couple hours."

---

6 Yeong-jin: Dad's Korean name, which Twig found on his diploma in his office. He goes by John, but Twig refuses to call him anything else, and I think Twig scares Dad, so he doesn't argue.

He sighed. "Natalie, I'm hearing what you're saying, and I know this has been really hard on you, but please understand—"

"Dad," I interrupted, "I'm hearing what *you're* saying, but this is for school. I really need to finish my lab report with Twig."

He was silent for a beat, and I could picture him running his left hand flat down the side of his face, debating. He used to do that when he thought about his research and his clients. Now he does it when he thinks about Mom and me.

In the end, his fatigue won over his desire to Therapist me. "Please be home for dinner?"

And then, simple as that, we were free to escape to Twig's place. It's only a fifteen-minute bike ride from the school. Ten if we're biking fast, and we rode fast today, trying to maximize our time together before Dad made me go home.

Twig and her mom live in this mansion of a house. Twig's dad is a banker in New York and makes buckets of money. Her parents are "amicably separated," but he sends these huge checks once a month, and Twig's mom makes a lot of money, too, designing apps that tell pretty people what clothes they should wear. Twig's mom is beautiful and used to be a supermodel, so she's basically obsessed with pretty clothes and pretty people, and they fly to Paris three times a year.[7]

Every time we pull up to her house on our bikes, I'm like, *Whoa.* We'll be biking along this tiny road covered in trees, and then out of nowhere their giant brick house will appear. Twig doesn't talk much about her parents, and she never brings anyone else to her house, which I guess isn't much of a problem because she doesn't have any friends besides me.

Here's the thing: Twig showed up in the middle of fourth grade. Like, one day she kind of *poof*ed in from a different universe. She wore an outfit entirely made of sequins to celebrate her first day and appeared as we all stood outside the classroom, waiting for school to start. Twig wore these plastic-heeled shoes that clacked when she walked, and everyone hushed and stared like we were in a movie. She laser-beamed over to Mikayla and me and said, "We're gonna be friends."

Mikayla made this weird, wrinkly look I'd never seen before and said, "Uh . . . ," but I smiled and said, "Awesome."

---

[7] Actually, Twig's mom is the one who named her, after some famous old supermodel. Everyone assumes *Twig* is a funny nickname because she's long and skinny and her ash-blond hair sticks out everywhere, but it's actually short for *Twiggy*. Twig's embarrassed about her name, so she doesn't bother correcting anyone.

Not everyone gets Twig—but I do.

Anyway, Twig and I rode in through the big gate to her house and tossed our bikes on the lawn. As soon as we walked inside, her housekeeper, Hélène, started fluttering around us. Hélène's from France, so she speaks with this fancy accent that Twig and I try to copy when she's not around. We don't do it in a mean way, though. We both really like Hélène.

"Natalie, is good to see my second-favorite girl," she said as she took our backpacks and hung them on the coatrack.

"Thanks, Hélène," I said. She poured us two tall glasses of cold milk, and Twig and I made our way down to the basement.[8]

"What should we play?" Twig asked as she flicked on the basement lights, illuminating our favorite hangout spot for the past few years. Two huge beanbags rested atop the hot-pink shag rug that Twig's mom hates but we love.

Twig walked over to the far wall and put a hand on her hip as she examined her huge bookshelf, filled entirely with board games. "We could play Sorry! or Parcheesi

---

8 Hélène's obsessed with milk. Every time I come over, the first thing she does is ask if I want milk. I don't even like milk, but I always end up drinking it at Twig's house because Hélène insists "ze bones must grow, ze bones must grow," and it's impossible to resist.

or Clue," she continued, but Twig only ever asks to seem polite. She always ends up picking the game herself.

"I don't care," I said, taking a sip of the milk and settling into the purple beanbag. By that point Twig had already pulled Clue out of her stack of a hundred billion board games and set it in front of me. She flopped onto the green bag and we set up the game, laying all the pieces out on the rug. We had this down to a science, and within a minute, Clue was ready.

We played twice; the second time we got Mrs. White with the candlestick in the kitchen, and the first time I don't remember. When Twig started resetting the pieces for the third time, I suggested we actually write our lab reports. She agreed reluctantly, then doodled all over the cover of her composition book.

"Doodles are an important part of the process," Twig said as she drew a row of cartwheeling frogs across the *NAME* line.

To be honest, I don't think I've ever seen her do homework, even though I know she's smart. School's not really something that concerns her, and she definitely doesn't care about this assignment.

But I spent an hour doing mine and writing all this because, I guess, for some reason, I kind of do.

ASSIGNMENT 4: PLANTS ARE PEOPLE, TOO

Mr. Neely must've gotten scared off by Mikayla's protest last week because today our assignment is boring. He walked around the classroom and handed out worksheets, which we're supposed to be silently filling out right now. It's just a giant picture of a plant, with little arrows and blanks where we're supposed to label the parts. I never thought I'd say this, but I miss cutting up dead frogs.

Even though I know how to fill out this worksheet, even though Mr. Neely's gone over the plant parts, and even though Mom has mentioned them more than a million times—I can't do it. Plants are a language I know, but thinking about them makes my stomach cramp, so I'm writing down my thoughts instead, just to look like I'm doing something.

Mikayla raises her hand and asks if this is a test, but Mr. Neely says, "Not a test for *me,* no! Not a test for a *grade*! But a test for *you,* to explore your own knowledge! A journey, a scientific quest," etc., etc.—you get the gist.

Dari's already done with his worksheet, of course, and I'm realizing now that the answers were probably in our reading from this weekend, which I didn't do. I haven't been doing much homework outside of this lab journal, and Dad doesn't bother me about it because he assumes I'm upset about Mom.

Here's a fun fact: Mom is a *botanist*. Or should I say: Mom used to be a botanist? I'm not sure, but before she got "sick," that was what she did. She worked for Mikayla's mom in a lab at Lancaster University and did all these scientific things, talking about plants and *genus* and *species* all the time. I know it sounds boring, but it wasn't. One time at dinner, Mom and Dad were talking about work, and they were going back and forth, laughing and joking like they used to, and Dad turned to me and said, "We're so different, your mom and me. I don't know the first thing about plants. I wouldn't know where to start."

But Mom shook her head and got serious and said, "That's not true. If you think about it, we do the same thing. You work with people and analyze how they think and feel, and I do the same—just with plants."

I laughed at that, but Dad stared at her in a way that said *I am so in love with you,* which made me want to gag and smile at the same time.

Looking back, I'm not so sure she was right. I want to say to her: *Plants are not people. Plants eat and grow and breathe, but they cannot laugh or sing or wonder.* And now *she* cannot laugh or sing or wonder.

I want to say to her: *Come back.*

Because maybe she is doing all of those laughing, crying things on the inside, just like her beloved plants, and she only needs someone to push her out, out, out again so she can laugh and sing and wonder on the outside, with me.

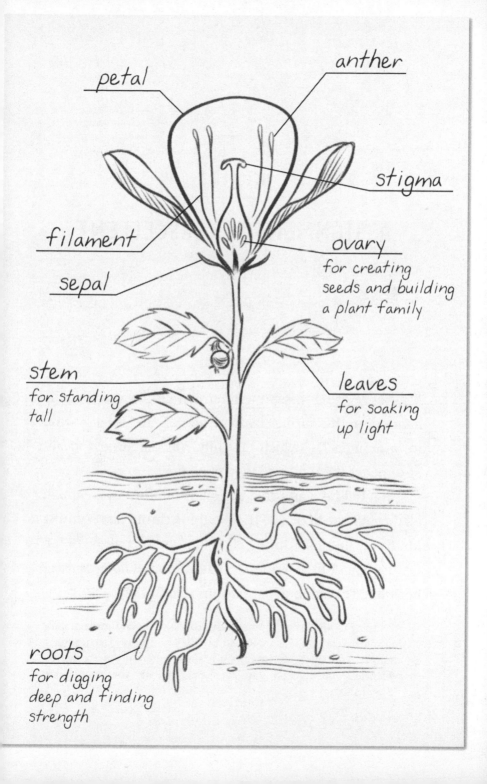

petal

anther

stigma

filament

sepal

ovary
for creating
seeds and building
a plant family

stem
for standing
tall

leaves
for soaking
up light

roots
for digging
deep and finding
strength

ASSIGNMENT 5: EGGSCELLENT

Mr. Neely asked to see me after class today. He actually announced this *during* class—"Natalie, can I speak to you for a moment?"—which not only was embarrassing but also meant there was no way to escape.

I figured he was going to yell at me for daydreaming all through the hour, so I tried to think through everything Mr. Neely had said during class, and I didn't get very far. On the board, he'd written the definition of *homeostasis*,[9] but I hadn't paid much attention beyond that.

---

9 According to Mr. Neely, "Homeostasis: this is your body's way of making sure everything runs smoothly! Even if your <u>external environment</u> changes, your body can maintain a stable <u>internal environment</u>— which lets you function, eat, sleep, play, and do your homework! #ThanksBody."

Mr. Neely didn't quiz me. Instead, he said, "I know you've been having trouble settling on a scientific question." He said this straight up, without any dorky exclamations or hashtags. "I thought you might be able to use a little help." He held out a yellow piece of paper: a flyer for a science competition. "I usually only recommend this to my top students, but I thought this might be good for you as well."

I'm pretty sure that was an insult, but I took the flyer anyway.

"There's no pressure, of course, but take a look. I think you might be interested, and I think you might surprise yourself." He smiled like he knew something I didn't, which is something I hate about adults. They always need to prove they're smarter than you. "Dari's doing it, too," Mr. Neely added. "Maybe you should work together. Science is always more fun with a friend."

Apparently, Mr. Neely didn't know me very well if he thought I'd be interested in doing extra homework and hanging out with super-genius Dari, but I nodded and forced a smile. "Um, thanks, I guess."

I glanced down at the flyer, which had a cheesy drawing of a giant smiling egg, with location and cash prize details underneath. I stuffed it into my backpack, knowing it would probably get crumpled with all the other random papers.

"Consider it," Mr. Neely said, still grinning way too

THE LANCASTER COUNTY YOUNG SCIENTIFIC MINDS ORGANIZATION...

THE EGG DROP!

WHAT: City wide egg drop contest for grades 6-8

WHY: To encourage the development of scientific potential in our children.

WHEN: January 13th, 1 pm

WHERE: 331 West Oak street, 3rd floor.

GRAND PRIZE: $500!!!!!

hard. "And if you decide not to use it for the Wonderings project, I do want you to come up with a different scientific question by the end of the month."

I thanked him again and left.

When I got home, I spent the rest of the day thinking about Mom. The old Mom would have loved this project. She would have sat with me for days, brainstorming different questions and experiments.

But that doesn't matter now. The old Mom has disappeared, replaced by someone I don't quite know—and for this project, I'm on my own.

ASSIGNMENT 6:
HOW TO GROW A MIRACLE

I'm not allowed in my parents' room. I used to be allowed, before this summer happened, when the door shut and stayed shut. Back then seems like a million months ago, even if it was just three.

It happened slowly. I didn't even notice the change at first—like when you grow out of your favorite jeans and you don't even realize how short they've gotten.

Mom started working less and sleeping more, and she wore pajamas around the house, which she'd never really done before. I was happy about this, at first. I thought it was a good thing, at first. I figured this meant she'd be around more, and we could hang out and talk, and she wouldn't have to go to the lab so much.

Only it didn't work out like that, obviously, and I didn't notice in time. Mom and Dad had been having whispered conversations at night, talking about problems at work, and I knew something was wrong, but I didn't know something was *Wrong*.

I didn't know until one dinner, when I finally understood: things were Not Okay. We were eating spaghetti and meatballs, only Dad had cooked, so it wasn't very good, and the air was thick and heavy with July heat. Dad made some joke and I laughed and Mom didn't.

And then I thought: *I can't remember the last time Mom laughed.*

I could hardly breathe, because I knew that something bad was happening, but I wasn't quite sure what.

Dad noticed, too, and his shoulders slumped, and his smile slipped away. It's the worst thing, to watch a smile fade like that.

The next morning, when I came downstairs, my parents' bedroom door was shut, and Dad was sitting at the kitchen table, by himself. I started walking toward their bedroom, but Dad stopped me before I could get any closer. I could tell he was as sad as I was, but he didn't say why.

"We'll be okay," he said, "but why don't you give your mother some space for now?"

And just like that, I wasn't allowed in their bedroom anymore. Dad put on a happy face and tried to be Normal

Dad, and Mom disappeared into that dark bedroom and became Not-Mom, and "Give your mother some space" became Dad's favorite phrase in the whole world.

But this evening, while Dad was holed up in his office and I should have been studying like a good daughter, I decided to break the rule.

I tiptoed past Dad's office and went to my parents' bedroom door, turning the knob slowly, pushing the door open, careful not to make any noise, barely even breathing. My heart beat in my ears, and sweat prickled against my palms, and I kind of hated Mom for *scaring* me. I kind of hated myself, too, for being scared.

Therapist Dad could probably dissect my whole heart based on that one little feeling, because who in the world is afraid of their own mother?

I took two quick, quiet breaths and told myself I was there for a reason. I still had to think of a scientific question, and maybe I could get some ideas from one of Mom's books. I didn't look at the lump on the bed that was Not-Mom. I just walked straight to the far wall of the room, to my parents' bookshelf.

Quick, Natalie. Quiet, Natalie.

The room was dark, but strands of light streamed in through the blinds—cracks of brightness and swirling dust in the midst of all this empty—and I could read the titles on the bookshelf. Mom has this one book, *Basic*

Botany, that she used to read to me, and I meant to reach for that one, but my hand fell on another book instead. Mom's book. *How to Grow a Miracle,* the book she hated because she wrote it ten years ago.

She told Dad once that she sounded young and naive, but I loved the way her paragraphs sounded—the way the botany-speak blended with her excitement and became a secret language with magic words. She wrote like it was a fairy tale, and reading those pages felt like peeking into the Mom of ten years ago: the Mom who wrote a book and nursed a baby. The Mom who loved growing things.

In the semidarkness of my parents' bedroom, I flipped the pages to the table of contents. Her book was divided into three sections, for three miracle plant stories, and the biggest section by far was the last:

The Cobalt Blue Orchid: The Flower of Mystery and Miracles.

I'd read this section over and over, but seeing those words now sent my heart whirring. Ideas and hope started sparking together inside me, reminding me of the way my mother used to be—excited by science and life and questions. I shut the book because I felt like I was on the brink of something dangerous, and if I took one step further, I'd never be able to go back.

I cradled the book to my chest and turned to watch

Mom as she slept, dark and dead to the world. I told myself to put the book back on the shelf, to go back to my homework and stop thinking about the miracle orchids.

But instead, I tucked the book under my shirt and left the room. It's not like I was going to read it. I just wasn't ready to put it back.

STEP 3:
INVESTIGATIVE RESEARCH

Grab your magnifying glass and your decoder ring because you're going to be investigating! Investigating *science*, that is. You'll all be researching your question, because research is fun, fun, fun! #SherlocksScientificProcess

ASSIGNMENT 7: EDUCATIONAL ADVENTURES IN BOARD GAME LAND

Mr. Neely showed a movie about fungus today, which meant half the class fell asleep immediately. It didn't help that rain drummed against the windows, a dreamy kind of lullaby that made it hard to concentrate. And even though I tried to focus on the fungi, my thoughts kept drifting back to the orchid and Mom's book.

I was so distracted that I almost didn't notice when Tom K. dropped a note on my desk. He pointed across the room at Twig when I looked up, and Twig nodded as I unfolded the note.

What's wrong?

I shrugged and crumpled the scrap of paper.

Twig frowned and sent another note down the line. Tom K. handed it to me, shooting me a look that said he didn't appreciate being our postman.

> *Don't shrug at me, Natalie. I can tell*
> *something's wrong. You look mopey.*

I shrugged again. Twig sent another note.

> *Now you're just being annoying. Come*
> *over after school? I got a new board*
> *game. Found it at a thrift store with*
> *Hélène. Called "Whose PANTS?" Needs to*
> *be played ASAP.*

And that's how I ended up back at Twig's house this afternoon, playing Whose PANTS? and having no idea whatsoever about our assignment for class. Between passing notes with Twig and thinking about Mom, I hadn't exactly paid attention in any of my classes.

"Were you listening when Mr. Neely explained the assignment?" I asked Twig as she rolled the dice and moved her little bell-bottom game piece across the board. As it turns out, Whose PANTS? is basically a combination of Guess Who? and Chutes and Ladders. You move around the board and ask yes-or-no questions, and the first pair of pants to be reunited with its owner wins.

"No, I was busy asking you what's wrong," Twig said. "Which you never answered, by the way, even though something was *obviously* wrong. You were frowning all through class, and not even at Mikayla. Does my owner wear glasses?"

"No," I answered. "And nothing is wrong. I promise."

Twig gave me a look that said she didn't believe me, but she didn't push it. Once upon a time, Twig and I told each other everything, because we're best friends and that's what best friends do. Once upon a time, I would have answered, *Yes, something's wrong.* And I would have told her that Mom stopped getting out of bed, and Dad and I couldn't make her happy anymore—not even with chicken and pasta—and everything was different now.

Instead, I asked, "Is my owner human?" Because in case I forgot to mention, some of the pants wearers were vampires or aliens. Also one centaur, although why the centaur needed pants was unclear.

"No, not human," Twig replied.

I had been heading down a path toward the clown (decidedly human), so I rolled the dice and started back-tracking.

Twig appeared in my life at the perfect time, back when Mikayla was getting weird—and our best-friendship was instant. Back then, I would have told Twig everything, and Twig would have said, *Tell me more,* and we would have talked and talked until my throat was scratched and raw with honesty.

But then we got older and Twig's parents got "amicably separated" and we learned which topics to avoid, because sometimes that's what best friends do, too.

Twig found her pants owner first, reuniting her bell-bottoms with the astronaut. She did her little celebratory dance, which consisted of lots of jumps and spins, but she seemed less enthusiastic than usual. For a second, I thought she might say something real, but then she saw the look on my face and said, "Let's play again."

ASSIGNMENT 8: THINGS I KNOW, THAT MY PARENTS THINK I DON'T KNOW

Before a scientist can understand what they *don't* know, they have to investigate what they *do* know. That was practically Mom's favorite rule of science, and whenever she tried to work through a Big Question, she always started by making a list of knowns. So here's what I know:

1. Mom and Dad met in college, and Dad fell in love first. I've seen their photo albums and it's stamped like *bam!* all over his face.

2. Mom is not beautiful, not in the usual way, but people always fall in love with her. She

had this *way* about her. Something like happiness.

3. Just a few months ago, over the summer, Mom was Mom. She was happy. She talked about her work at the university lab, the research with the orchids and potential breakthroughs, and she smiled and things were good.

4. And then the hushed conversations started. *Not enough funding, not enough findings.* Again and again and again. And one conversation, in particular: *She thinks I should take a break.* I played all those snippets over again in my head after things got really bad, looking for some kind of explanation. And then it clicked. Mrs. Menzer fired Mom. This was the woman I'd known all my life, who'd worked by Mom's side and laughed as Mikayla and I presented fake research reports. The woman who'd come to our house for countless dinners, who'd always asked me about my life as if she actually cared. But after ten years of research, she stopped believing in the Cobalt Blue Orchids. And she stopped believing in Mom. I don't know which betrayal is worse.

5. Mom couldn't go to work anymore, and she got sucked into the darkness. Basically, Mrs. Menzer ruined our lives, because it was like she broke Mom. Mom just *stopped*. And now I don't know what to do. I don't know how to fix her.

ASSIGNMENT 9: INVESTIGATIVE RESEARCH

Mr. Neely has decided to give us a break from cutting open small animals and watching boring videos to return to the scientific process. He reminded us to keep working on our long-term project. He also gave me a "friendly reminder" to find a question to investigate.

Question: At what temperature does water boil?

Answer: 212 degrees Fahrenheit, 100 degrees Celsius, according to Google. #Done.

And because I finished my homework early, I figured I might as well investigate my secret question—the question I couldn't find the words for.

I let myself into Dad's office. He sat with his back to me, hunched over a bunch of files on his desk. His office is bright, with big floor-length windows and lamps—lots of lamps. He's all about brightness now that Mom has retreated into the dark.

"Dad?" I walked up behind him, feeling like a shadow.

He startled a bit and turned around, blinking at me like his eyes were adjusting. "Hello, Natalie, what is it?" he said, all formal and weird, like he always gets when he's working.

"I'm doing research for class," I said.

He glanced down at my notebook and relaxed because research is where Dad's most comfortable. He's safe inside statistics and diagnoses and actionable next steps. I looked down at my notebook, got my pen ready to show him this was strictly business, and continued. "What does it mean if someone only likes to be in the dark?"

I could tell he saw right through me because he tensed back up again. "Naaaatalie," he said, drawing my name out, cautious.

I pressed on, staring back down at my notebook, because I didn't really want to know the answers, but also, I really did. "Why would somebody stop caring about their family?" I asked.

"Natalie," Dad said again. He nudged my notebook away so he could look me right in the eyes. Dad believes in eye contact. "We should talk about your mother. We should talk about how you're feeling."

I told him I didn't want to talk about my mother, or

my feelings. What I wanted was to finish my science assignment. But Dad was looking at me with those Therapist Eyes, saying, "I want you to know: what's happening with your mother has nothing to do with you."

That's the problem. I don't seem to affect her at all. And that has *everything* to do with me. Of course, I couldn't tell him that, so I said, "Never mind," and left his office. He was conflicted, I could tell, but he didn't follow me.

I didn't know where to go then. I felt trapped between the dark of Mom's room and the fake light of Dad's office, and without thinking, I went to my bedroom, grabbed Mom's book, and walked right outside, into Mom's greenhouse.

My earliest memories are of being in that greenhouse with Mom, growing our little plant family, following her rules, watering and fertilizing each seed just right. A few months earlier, the greenhouse had been beautiful, blooming with life and color and real, delicious light.

It was less beautiful now. In the summer, when Mom stopped working, *caring,* Dad went into a frenzy over the flowers, brimming with energy I'd never seen in him, watering and weeding and watering some more. Dad spent hours in the greenhouse trying to save the plants my mother no longer loved.

He loved them too hard, if you know what I mean, if you know plants at all. Some of them survived, but you're not supposed to water plants too much. They need *space*. Funny, huh?

Mom and I used to spend all our time in here, touching and smelling the flowers, talking about life, and soaking up sunlight. But today I stood in the corner for the first time in six weeks, staring at our used-to-be plants—brown and crisp and dead all over.

In the center of the greenhouse, one tall stem stood alone, brown like all the rest of the plants. The petals had long abandoned it. But it used to be blue—a brilliant, magic kind of blue. A Cobalt Blue Orchid. A plant with a brand-new Latin name.[10] A miracle plant all our own.

I sat down on the dirt floor, beneath the row of dead plants so I couldn't see them, and held Mom's book in my lap. I didn't mean to read it. I meant to turn around and go back inside, but my hands opened the book almost without meaning to. That excited-nervous feeling came back as I smelled its old-book smell, and I turned to the Cobalt Blue Orchid section and read Mom's words.

> In San Juan, New Mexico, in 1991, a pipe at a
> power plant burst. The town was contaminated
> with toxic amounts of metal and chemicals in
> the soil, but all the people were safe.

---

10   Family: Orchidaceae, for orchid. Genus: *Cattleya,* for the botanist William Cattley. Species: *fortis,* for brave.

The flowers were not. All the flowers died—every last one. Toxic amounts of cobalt and aluminum saturated the earth, poisoning the plants. Nothing could grow, and nothing did grow.

Until two years later, seemingly out of nowhere, an orchid sprouted, a shock of blue in this vast expanse of empty dirt. Not too long after, another emerged. Soon enough, there were bright blue orchids blooming all over the field.

Imagine it. Imagine driving past this field of dirt every day on your way to work, past all that nothingness, and then one day: flowers. Beautiful blue flowers everywhere.

First nothing, then everything.

I read on, past Mom's chapter on *anthocyanin pigments* and *active ion transport,* past her talk of hybrids and fungus and moss. The sun started slipping away, and the light in the greenhouse faded. I kept expecting Dad to come find me, to tell me to come inside for dinner, but he never came. And I kept reading:

Perhaps you have to be a botanist to understand the significance of these Cobalt Blue Orchids—to know how delicate orchids are.

How they die without the perfect amount of sun and just the right amount of water. And you would have to understand the sheer impossibility of a blue orchid in order to understand the miracle of these flowers. How this delicate orchid somehow sprouted when no other plant could. How it sucked those toxic chemicals straight out of the earth and churned them into beauty.

But I'd like to think that even without knowing the nitty-gritty of how plants work, all you'd have to do is stand in the middle of that shockingly blue field to know that this is science at its most miraculous—its most magical.

Mom was the one who believed in this flower—in all it could do. She'd told the story a million times. How everyone was shocked and amazed by the color.[11] How all the other botanists studied the blueness, but Mom said, *Wait. There's more.* There was a magic in living through that chemical poison, and Mom was the first one to realize it.

---

11 For those of you who haven't spent your whole life with a botanist mother, orchids don't grow blue in nature. You can dye them blue, but they don't grow that way. And then the disaster happened and orchids started growing, sucking up the processed chemicals from moss, and just like that: blue orchid. Ta-da, magic. Science. Miracle.

And while Mom and Mrs. Menzer studied the Cobalt Blue Orchid in their lab, Mom and I kept our own orchid in the greenhouse. We nurtured it and cared for it and loved it. We kept it safe.

And now it's dead. My mother—the one who once wrote about science and magic and miracles—let it die. I felt that whirring, sparking feeling in my chest again. An idea was starting to click into place.

Because even though our orchid was dead, there was still that vast, beautiful field of blue all the way in New Mexico, full of miracles and hope. Maybe Mom just needed to be reminded of that.

Maybe she'd forgotten.

STEP 4: HYPOTHESIS

A *hypothesis* is an *educated guess*! And since you're all *educated* and good at *guessing*, this assignment is *perfect* for you! Time to put those ol' brainz to the test!
#EducatedStudentz

ASSIGNMENT 10: MEIOSIS AND MR. POTATO HEAD

Mom and I had a Halloween tradition. Every year, I would dress up as a different plant. I would flip through her botany books to find the perfect one, and we'd go to the craft store together and make an elaborate costume. Last year, I dressed as the Hawaiian hāpuʻu pulu fern, and Mom and I spent hours making huge spiraling fronds that came up off my shoulders. Most people thought I was some kind of alien or insect, but I didn't even care, and Twig and I walked all through my neighborhood trick-or-treating.

Add Halloween to the list of things Mom forgot to care about, because this year, she didn't mention it. So I didn't, either, and Dad didn't, and our whole family spent this past week carefully avoiding the subject.

I came downstairs this morning in regular clothes, my normal jeans and a plain sweater. When Dad looked up at me, sadness flashed across his face—just for a moment, and then it was gone. "No costume this year, Nats?" His voice was all false cheerfulness. "You know, there's still time to dig that fern costume out of the garage, if you're up for it."

I half shrugged, half shook my head. "I'm too old for costumes now," I said.

I told myself this was true. That I wouldn't have worn a costume anyway. If Twig had been in town, she would have protested and worn the flashiest costume she could find—probably something that lit up or made noise—but she was in Paris with her mom for the week.[12]

Thing is: I kind of *was* too old, for the most part. A handful of kids dressed up today, but most kids just wore normal clothes, or those don't-actually-count costumes like baseball jerseys.

"I haven't dressed up in *three years*," I overheard

---

12 Twig complained about this, if you can believe it. "It's one of those brainwashing things," she told me. "My mom is going to force me to sit through all those shows and watch tall girls walk back and forth, and then we're going to go eat little cakes with her friends and talk about clothing." As if tall girls and cakes and clothes were the worst things in the world. Sometimes I don't understand Twig at all.

Mikayla tell Janie as I shoved my books into my locker before class. She said it as if this were something to brag about, and I bit the inside of my cheek and tried not to think about what plant Mom and I might have chosen this year.

Mostly, I spent the day keeping my head down and trying not to think too hard about stuff, which I guess is kind of becoming my pattern. I was doing a pretty good job of avoiding any attention until the end of the day.

Mr. Neely asked to speak to me after class. Again. Which was pretty embarrassing. And when he finally let us go for the day, I spent as long as possible packing up my books, trying to delay the awkwardness of having to talk to him. Mikayla raised her eyebrows at me as she left, like, *Boy, you must be really stupid.* I hate that I was once best friends with her.

After everybody had bolted, I shuffled up to Mr. Neely's desk. "Hi," I said, which sounded just as awkward as I'd expected, but I wasn't sure what else to say.

We're studying cell division right now, so for Halloween he dressed up as meiosis. This pretty much meant he was wearing a giant Velcro vest with little chromosomes attached. He'd been rearranging them during class, using the vest to demonstrate all the different phases of cell division. He was also inexplicably wearing ladybug antennae. I don't even know.

57

He pointed to his vest, all excited. "Hey, can you tell me which phase of meiosis this cell is currently in?"

I stared at his vest. One of the chromosomes wasn't sticking to the Velcro very well, so it drooped a little. It had been bothering me the whole time.

"Um," I said. "I *hypothesize* that it's . . . micro . . . phase?" I don't think he was trying to test me, but it was pretty clear I hadn't been paying attention.

Mr. Neely deflated a bit. "Well, good job hashtag-educated-guessing, but it's actually telophase two. See, the chromosomes have been divided into four separate haploids."

"Oh, right." I nodded as if I understood what he was talking about. "Um, is that why you called me up here?" I asked, even though I knew exactly why he wanted to talk to me.

"Not quite." He smiled at me, one of those *you're not in trouble yet but you will be soon* smiles that teachers love to give. "Have you thought any more about your scientific question?"

I'd been thinking a lot about Mom, and I had about a million half questions swirling in my head about her, but that wasn't what he was looking for. "Uh," I said.

He nodded very slowly and examined me. I hate how adults look at me now, ever since the "situation" started.

"Well, you know I'd love for you to do the egg drop,"

he said, "but whatever it is, you need to pick something by Friday. If you're having any trouble, I suggest starting back at the scientific process. Use your Wonderings journal to plumb the depths of thinking, to observe and question the world." He winked—actually winked—so I knew Mr. Neely was back to being weird old Mr. Neely and not one of those teachers who *examined* their students.

"Okay, will do," I said, but that sounded kind of rude, so I added, "Thanks for the suggestion."

He grinned like I'd just thrown a parade in his honor. "You're so very welcome, Natalie!"

And how do you even respond to that? I smiled and left.

Everyone else had left by then, too, rushing off to see scary movies or pass out candy or go trick-or-treating or whatever they happened to have planned for Halloween. The hallway was practically deserted—all except for Dari, that is, who was sitting by the lockers. He was reading a textbook, advanced something-something. He was also dressed as a giant potato.

He looked up when he saw me leaving Mr. Neely's classroom and shifted in his homemade potato. It crinkled, as if it was stuffed with old newspapers. The costume practically swallowed him up, and his head looked tiny compared to the horror that took up his midsection. He stood up as I passed, and his costume shifted from side to side, throwing him off balance so he wobbled a little.

"What were you guys talking about?" he asked, speaking even faster than usual, as if he was concerned—or jealous.

"Oh, you know, just Mr. Neely stuff." I wondered if I should ask about the potato, or if I should wait for him to bring it up, or if maybe we shouldn't acknowledge it at all.

But Dari looked at me like I was the one being weird, like he was waiting for me to finish my sentence. "Well, just, you know." Dari kept waiting, and I realized there wasn't a non-awkward way to get out of this. "We talked about the *joys of science!*" I did my best Mr. Neely impression, clasping my hands together while making my eyes go big and emphasizing *Every. Single. Word.*

That made Dari smile. "You know he does try. He's a smart guy and he cares."

I'd never heard a kid talk about a teacher that way. The words seemed too friendly. *Dari* seemed too friendly— we'd never actually spoken before, but here we were, chatting away while he sat there in a potato. The weird part: I was kind of enjoying it.

"He had a boring job before he switched to teaching, so he's just excited to be here," he said.

I nodded as if I'd already known that factoid. It made sense—Mr. Neely didn't look young enough to be a new teacher, but he wasn't *old,* either.

But the way Dari talked about Mr. Neely was strange,

like they were actually friends. I changed the subject. "Why are you still at school?"

Dari raised his textbook as if that answered my question: ADVANCED ALGEBRA.

"Well, yeah, but why are you still *here*? Nobody stays late after school." I wanted to add: *Especially not on Halloween. Especially not while they're wearing a potato.* But I didn't. I felt like I'd missed the opportunity to say something about the costume, and if I said something now it would seem like I was making fun of him.

Dari shrugged, pressing his bony shoulders all the way up to his ears. The potato crinkled and bobbed. "My parents work late. They can't pick me up until seven."

"Oh."

"But when they come, we're going to take a haunted hayride. It's going to be fun." I liked the way he spoke, all crisp and sharp. He carried the smallest trace of an accent, and his words sounded like they were walking along the countryside, up and down and up and down the hills. And then I felt guilty for being so *aware* of his Indianness, like I was judging him, even though I wasn't.

"So," I said, since he was the one who brought up Halloween. "The potato?"

"Is it weird?" He didn't sound defensive or self-conscious. He sounded like he was asking a scientific question and wanted to investigate.

"Um," I said, wanting to be nice but not wanting to

lie. "I guess I assumed you'd dress up as an atom or an equation or something."

Dari laughed. When I looked closer at the potato, I realized that what I thought were random squiggles—potato eyes or globs of dirt, or something—were actually small drawings: a pair of lips, an ear, what I assumed was probably a nose.

"It's a mixed-up Mr. Potato Head," he explained, with a whole lot of pride in his voice and no embarrassment at all. "It was my older brother's, when he was in middle school. I helped him make it for a costume contest. See, I drew the mustache." He pointed to a squiggly black line near his hip.

"Oh," I said. I couldn't help but think about how much Twig would have loved a mixed-up Mr. Potato Head costume, in all its weirdness, and I made a mental note to tell her when she got back.

Dari kept going. "We forgot about the costume, but we found it when we moved to America a few years ago. I think it makes my parents happy to see me wearing it. It brings them back, you know?"

I tried to imagine myself dressed up as a Cobalt Blue Orchid. If Mom saw a costume like that, would it make a difference? Would it bring her back? "So, seeing you as a potato makes them happy?"

Dari shrugged. The potato crinkled again. "I think just

seeing the potato itself. It reminds them of how happy we all were when we made it."

"Oh," I said again. "Well, I like it."

Dari smiled, and I smiled back, and there was a long silence where neither of us had anything else to say. I shifted my backpack on my shoulders. "Well, I better go, since, you know, I'm not a weirdo who hangs around in a potato after school."

He laughed as if I'd made a joke.

And I guess I had.

ASSIGNMENT 11: DECISIONS

I woke up this morning all alive with a new idea and filled with hope, and I ran to wake Mom. I wanted her to be alive with me.

Dad was downstairs, packing up my lunch and getting ready for work, and I had to tiptoe very quietly toward their room, so he wouldn't stop me in my tracks and turn me right around.

"Mom," I said, curling up next to her on the bed.

She rolled around and smiled at me, her eyes bleary with sleep. She seemed happy, or at least content.

"Mom, I had an idea," I said. I was already dressed in my school clothes, and she was in her pajamas, and everything felt backward, but I focused on my plan and tried not to think of everything that was wrong.

"What's that, Nats?" She didn't say it any particular way, but somehow, there was a shift in the air, like she'd been there for a moment, and all of a sudden I was losing her again.

"The Cobalt Blue Orchids, in New Mexico," I told her. I still felt excited by the possibility, like if I reminded her about the flowers, she'd wake up and say, *Of course!*— like if she just saw that orchid field again, she'd remember who she was. I could bring her back.

"We have to go," I said. "You told me you'd take me but you never did, and now our orchid is dead, and we should go get a new one. You have to *see* the orchids. And then—"

"Our orchid?" she asked. Mom's eyes were blue, but they looked gray in the dark. "What are you talking about?"

Suddenly this felt like a huge mistake. She hadn't known that the orchid was dead—how had she not known? How long had it been since she was in the greenhouse?

"But we can get a new one," I pushed on. "In New Mexico."

She looked so lost, and I thought she wouldn't say anything at all, but then she said, "Okay."

I bit my cheek, trying to push down that hope that was building inside me. "Really?" My voice came out as a whisper, even though I hadn't meant it to.

"When we have the money, Natalie," she sighed, and closed her eyes, and I wanted to shake her and say, *Stay awake! For one moment just stay awake, notice your dying flowers. Notice me!*

"We just don't have the money for travel right now," she repeated, eyes still closed.

I slipped back out of the bed and walked out of the room, tripping over the dresser as I made my way through the darkness. I chewed on my cheek until the fleshy part was raw, and went to pack my backpack for school, because today was just another day.

Not such a brand-new, hopeful day after all.

But here's the thing. When I glanced down in my bag, my eyes caught on that crumpled-up piece of bright yellow paper, and my hope flared up again. I reached in and pulled out Mr. Neely's flyer, scanning straight past the happy egg to the bottom. And there, in big, bold letters and everything:

GRAND PRIZE: $500!!!!!

Seeing those letters, that big, fat money prize, I felt like I'd been falling into some deep, hopeless black hole, and the universe looked at me and said, *Not yet, Natalie. Don't give up yet.*

A million years ago, when I was about five, I got sick in the wintertime. Not the sniffly kind of winter-sick that everyone gets when the leaves change colors, but a real kind of sick.

I slept through the winter, the way plants hibernate. I slept and the house turned dark and silent, but Mom lay next to me, refusing to leave my side. And then spring came, and I woke up with all those brand-new blooming buds. I don't remember much about the illness or the recovery. I only remember waking up. And I remember Mom waking with me.

Dad and I never talk about that time. We don't talk about how we're leaving Mom alone now. We don't talk about how to cure her.

We hardly talk at all.

But I remember, and I know we can't give up on her. She never gave up on me.

I took the flyer and I decided, right then and there: I'm not leaving Mom alone. I will win the money, and Mom and I will fly to New Mexico. We'll pick one of those magical blue flowers, and Mom and I will study it, and everything will go back to normal. Everything will be perfect.

ASSIGNMENT 12: THE EGG LIST HYPOTHESIS

The contest was about two months away, right after winter break, so I had to start as soon as possible. I figured, *This can't be that hard. I'll just sandwich the egg in a bunch of pillows.* But when I started reading about the contest online, things got a little more complicated.

Issue #1: The Lancaster County Young Scientific Minds Organization's website is ancient. I'm talking *last updated in 2003* ancient, so it's hard to navigate and find all the rules.

Issue #2: As it turns out, this whole egg drop thing is more than just wrapping up an egg in pillows. Not only do they drop the egg from three stories up, but they also have a point system for things like *bounce factor* and *aerodynamic design.* I'm starting to think I should've left this project for Mr. Neely's "top students," but then again, five hundred dollars. Five hundred dollars that might bring Mom back.

I made up a list of materials and took it to Dad, who was in the kitchen again. He's been in the kitchen a lot lately. When Mom was, well, Mom, she loved cooking. She would blast eighties music and zip between the stove and the cutting board and the oven. Sometimes I would help her, and we'd always end up singing into our spatulas and dancing around to some Bon Jovi song.

Dad doesn't play music when he cooks.

"I made a list," I said.

Dad turned around and he had flour spilled all down the front of his shirt, and I snorted, because I didn't think Dad in the kitchen would ever stop being ridiculous.

"A list?" he asked.

"Yeah. What are you doing?" I asked, waving my hands at the flour mess.

He wiped his hands on his jeans, which didn't help, since flour coated his jeans, too. "I'm practicing—trying to make Grandma's cran-apple pie."

It took me a second to realize that by "Grandma" he meant *Mom's* mom, because Dad's mom only cooks Korean food and chicken nuggets.[13] Which meant this was the pie Mom made for Thanksgiving every year after her mother died. The one I always helped her make.

I felt very sad all of a sudden.

Dad must've noticed, because he walked over and took the list from my hands. "Eggs? Are you baking your own pie?" He half laughed at his joke, even though it wasn't funny. "Bubble Wrap? Parachutes? Play-Doh?"

The Play-Doh was a shot in the dark. "It's for school," I said.

"Ah." He nodded and got excited in that embarrassing way parents get when they try to Be Involved in Their Kids' Lives and also possibly try to Distract Them from Their MIA Mother. "The egg drop! I remember that! Of course we can pick these things up. What's your plan?"

"I don't really have a plan," I said. I didn't feel all that excited about the egg drop anymore.

Dad hesitated. "Do you want to help me with my pie?"

I wanted to scream at him for even thinking of taking Mom's pie and making it *his*. But I just said, "Thanksgiving's still, like, a month away." I tried to sound ca-

---

13 Apparently, when Dad was a kid, he went through a phase where he ate only chicken nuggets. This information comes in handy when he pesters me to finish my vegetables.

sual, like I didn't care, like I was only stating a fact, but my voice wobbled and I could feel my eyes stinging. I wanted to catch all those feelings before they escaped and force them down. I wrapped my arms around myself, crossing them over my chest.

It didn't take Dad long to morph into Therapist Dad.[14]

"Natalie, why don't you have a seat?" He gestured to our dining table.

I stayed standing.

Dad went on, "I think it might be best for you to see someone outside the family. That way, you can talk freely." He looked so lost telling me what to do. That had always been Mom's job—bossing us around—and we'd let her, because she'd always done a pretty good job of it.

I held up my list. "I have to focus on the egg thing, Dad."

The muscles between his eyebrows twitched. "Okay, the pie can wait. If we go pick up the items on your list, will you let me schedule an appointment for you to meet with someone?"

I wanted to tell him no, because the thing was, I didn't have anything to say. He acts like I bottled everything up inside, but really, I'm okay. I'm fine. "Yeah, sure, Dad," I said.

---

14 Therapist Dad, *n.:* pinched eyebrows, lowered voice, lots of questions, feared by daughters everywhere.

So we went to pick up eggs, and Dad got distracted pretty fast, asking all these questions about the egg drop, etc., etc., etc. I answered everything and acted all excited, but here's a *hypothesis:* Adults don't want to know how we're feeling. They think they do, but really, they just want to believe we're okay, because it makes their job easier. Dad and I talked a whole lot about the egg drop list, but we weren't *talking,* not really.

ASSIGNMENT 13: OPERATION EGG

Twig enlisted herself to help with the whole egg thing. Only, Rule #1 of Twig's help: Stop calling it "the whole egg thing."

"It sounds boring," she shouted from up ahead as we biked to her house after school.

"It *is* boring," I said. "It's for school."

"Not if I'm helping. From now on, we will hereby refer to it as Operation Egg."

"Fine. Operation Egg it is." It kind of had a ring to it, even if it was a little kid-ish. *Operation Egg* made this feel important. It *was* important.

Mr. Neely had practically burst with joy when I told

him I'd chosen the egg competition for my Wonderings project, and he allowed Twig to work on it, too, as long as we investigated different questions.[15]

"You can both take different approaches to the project," he had explained. "For example, one of you could study velocity—"

"I call velocity!" Twig had shouted, and it had been decided. I still didn't know my own question, but I'd figure that out later.

"Hey, Natalie," Twig said as we pedaled down the long road that led to her house. "Check out my velocity." And then she pumped her fist in the air and her bike teetered for a moment before she leaned forward and pedaled faster, leaving me behind.

When I finally made it to Twig's mansion, she was already sitting at the kitchen table. She raised an eyebrow and smirked at me. "I've been waiting for ages," she said, lifting her hand to her mouth and fake-yawning—but her cheeks were flushed and her chest was rising and falling. Twig's not the best actress, to be honest.

"Natalie!" Twig's mother floated into the kitchen as I sat down across from Twig. I'm not kidding, the woman

---

[15] Twig gladly abandoned her original question—something with food coloring and placebo effects. "It was boring," she said, because Twig doesn't care for long-term projects. She likes jumping to the next thing.

seems to float everywhere, as if she's too posh to walk like all of us peasants. "How lovely to see you."

According to Twig, she and her mom had a huge fight in Paris. Twig had insisted on dressing as an evil witch/candy cane hybrid for Halloween,[16] even though nobody really celebrates Halloween in France, and Twig's mom said she was being embarrassing. Long story short, their trip was a disaster. But the way Twig's mom smiled at me, it was as if nothing bad had ever happened. She's a better actress than Twig, but I guess she's had more years of practice. Adults are good at pretending.

"Nice to see you, too," I said, and when Twig's mom raised an expectant eyebrow, I added, "Clarissa."

Twig's mom insists that everyone, including Twig, call her by her first name.

"And how is your family?" Clarissa asked. "I haven't seen your mom in a while. She works so hard."

I bit my lip and tried to nod.

"I really should give her a call. You know, us working girls have to stick together." She flashed a smile as my stomach twisted.

"Mom," Twig said, shooting Clarissa a *what are you even saying* look.

At school, Twig's always crawling around under desks,

---

16 Don't ask.

pretending to be a secret agent spy or something weird like that, but when her mother's around, Twig turns into one of those embarrassed sitcom-type twelve-year-olds.

When her mother's around, Twig becomes almost normal. And I'm not sure how to feel about that.

"Okay, okay." Clarissa cleared her throat, faked a smile, and gave a high-pitched glittery laugh. "I have to run to my office anyway. Ask Hélène if you want some milk."

Twig glared at her mom and I gave a little wave goodbye. Clarissa glitter-laughed again and floated away.

When we were alone, Twig frowned. "Sorry about her," she said.

If I were Twig, I wouldn't apologize for Clarissa, because at least she was walking around and talking and *living*—but I kept my mouth shut. Twig knew Mom wasn't working anymore, but that was all she knew. The topic was one of those No-Go Zones.

"So, anyway. Operation Egg," she said in a Serious Business voice. "What's the plan?"

I sighed. First Dad, now Twig—everyone expected me to have a plan. I reached into my backpack and pulled out my list. "My dad and I bought this stuff a few days ago."

"Sweet." She took the list from me and read it. Her eyes moved over the items, as if this whole egg thing—or

Operation Egg—were one of her games. Soon she would be talking strategy and battle moves and breaking out her dice, just for luck. "Play-Doh?"

I shrugged. "I thought it might help."

She scrunched up her face and then nodded. "Yes, I like it. *Basketball?*"

"I thought that might help, too?"

Twig laughed, slapping the table so hard the glasses jumped. Nobody could laugh like Twig. "Why on earth would you think that?"

My cheeks got hot, and my eyes burned, even though this was only Twig, even though she hadn't meant to say anything wrong. "I thought maybe I could put the egg inside it," I said.

Twig frowned. Her tone softened. "How?"

"Um."

And then she tilted her head and squinted at me like I was her scientific question and she was trying to investigate the answer. "And your dad just bought all this stuff for you? He didn't think these items were a little weird?"

"I think he felt bad."

I could tell Twig was thinking, wondering what I wasn't saying, but she didn't ask.

Twig was good like that.

ASSIGNMENT 14: INVESTIGATIVE RESEARCH, AGAIN

After school, I went into Dad's office before he got home from his therapy sessions, sank into his big desk chair, and Googled egg drop ideas on his computer. *Investigative research,* Mr. Neely. I found things I had never thought of before—plastic bags and cotton balls and toothpicks and straws. I made a new list.

And when the office door opened, I knew it was her.

"What're you doing?" Mom asked.

I spun Dad's desk chair around to face her. Her eyes were red and blurry around the edges, as if she'd been sleeping for a thousand years. The orange of the setting sun lit her golden curls, unbrushed and unwashed, and her skin was paler than usual, but she looked like

Mom. Or she looked like Mom with something missing. I wanted to cry, but I didn't want to scare her away.

In her book, she'd written: *Science is living. Science is asking questions and finding answers and never, ever stopping.* I wanted to scream her own words at her, and I wanted to say, *Why did you stop?* But I didn't say that, either.

"It's for school," I said. I wish I could've said more—something about the orchids and the prize money—but I wasn't sure how. I needed to keep her here.

She walked over and started playing with my hair, so much darker than her own. I felt like I was five again. "'Egg drop designs'?" she read over my shoulder.

"Yeah, it's kind of silly."

For some reason, her touch wasn't comforting. I felt like I didn't know this person. My stomach twisted and I imagined myself standing up, sending the desk chair crashing into the wall. I imagined shoving this Not-Mom and screaming, *Give her back! Give her back to me!*

"Use cereal," she said. "Pack the egg in a plastic bag, surrounded with cereal. That's what I did when I was your age."

And then she left the office. I did not stand. I did not send the chair rolling back. I did not shove or scream or speak. My heart cracked at the sound of the door clicking shut, but I did not cry.

Instead, I added to my list: *cereal.*

STEP 5: PROCEDURE

Time to create a plan of action! How will your experiment work? Take a moment to lay out your steps. Remember: planning makes perfect! #PlanForPerfect

ASSIGNMENT 15:
BATTLE PLANS AND BEETLES

We had a half day of school today, the day before Thanksgiving, so Twig and I spent the afternoon comparing notes on Operation Egg. Twig had drawn a whole stack of egg drop designs and had started an Operation Egg binder, which contained all her notes and was covered in beetle stickers.[17] Twig's flying to New York to see her dad tomorrow, but she changes the subject anytime I mention it. And anyway, I had my own things I didn't want to discuss, so we poured ourselves into our science.

---

[17] Fifty cents at Paper World, according to Twig. So get 'em while the getting's good. That is, of course, if you're a weirdo who wants a jumbo pack of beetle stickers.

"You mentioned a basketball," she told me as she pushed one of her diagrams across the shag rug on her basement floor, "and I shouldn't have laughed. I've been thinking it could work. We cut a hole here, see? And we fill the rest with water. Then we can duct-tape the top back on. Did you know duct tape is awesome? We can use it for, like, everything."

I shifted on my purple beanbag. Hélène had the day off, and Clarissa was working double time to finish a new app update before Christmas, so it was just the two of us in this enormous house. Sometimes I had the urge to scream in Twig's house, just to see if I echoed.

"I guess the basketball could work," I said, even though I wasn't too sure. I appreciated her for being nice about the whole basketball idea, but the diagram looked pretty ridiculous, to be honest. I mean, it was an egg floating in a hollowed-out basketball.

"I have this one, too." Twig handed me a drawing of an egg covered in cotton balls. "First we cover the egg in Play-Doh, and then stick a bunch of cotton balls to the Play-Doh." When I was younger, Mom and I used to make Easter egg animals. We'd blow the yolks out of the eggs, and paint little faces on them. We made chicks, and bunnies, and lambs. The lambs, we covered in cotton balls.

"This could work," I told her as I examined her design. I meant it this time.

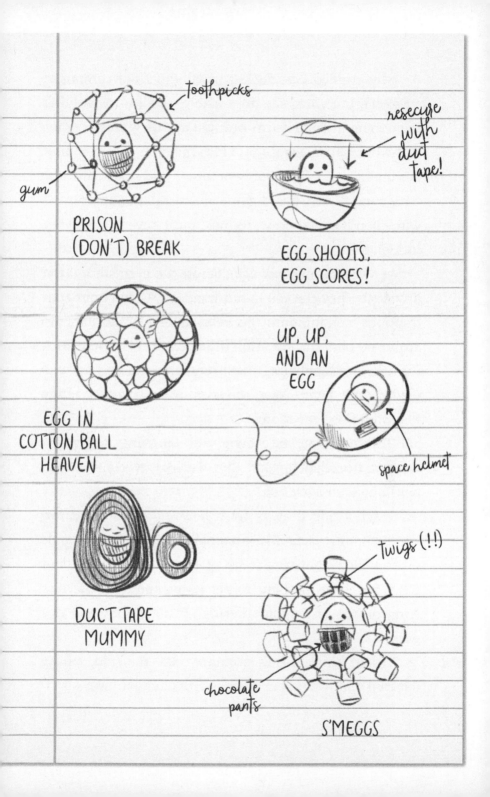

toothpicks

gum

PRISON
(DON'T) BREAK

resecure with duct tape!

EGG SHOOTS,
EGG SCORES!

EGG IN
COTTON BALL
HEAVEN

UP, UP,
AND AN
EGG

space helmet

DUCT TAPE
MUMMY

twigs (!!)

chocolate pants

S'MEGGS

Twig grinned. She doesn't usually focus or commit to a project, but when she does, she goes all in. She didn't seem to mind that I hadn't brought any diagrams or notes of my own. Twig always provides the momentum behind our operations. She is bold and brave and smart, and she wins almost every board game we ever play. Sometimes I win when it comes down to luck, but I haven't been very lucky lately.

We went through six eggs before we even started the drop test. They cracked in our hands as we built our contraptions, spilling onto the newspaper we had haphazardly laid out. The Play-Doh didn't work. We would stick it to the egg, apply too much pressure, and end up covered in yolk. Before long, the scent of raw egg and tangy Play-Doh filled the room.

"This smells *so bad*," Twig said, laughing as egg goo dripped from her fingers. She reached over and wiped her hand across my hair.

"Hey!" I pulled away from her, and she lunged forward, coming at me like a zombie with her eggy hands outstretched. "You're a freak of nature," I told her, but I was laughing too hard to get away, and then she was lying on top of me, smothering me in giggles and egg guts.

"I don't think this is gonna work," she said, sitting back up and wiping her hands across her corduroys.

"We might need to rethink this one," I agreed.

"Also, we probably should've done this outside. I guess we better start cleaning," Twig said as she surveyed the destroyed shag rug in the basement. At least Clarissa wouldn't be upset about throwing it out.

She ran upstairs to grab paper towels and Clorox wipes and maybe some Febreze, and I sat with our fallen soldiers. I don't know why I didn't tell Twig about Mom's cereal idea. I think I wanted to keep that to myself for a while.

ASSIGNMENT 16: TURKEY DAY

Mom was in the kitchen when I went downstairs this morning, sifting flour into a mixing bowl. Her hair was washed, and she was wearing her favorite sundress, the one with blue stars.

"Good morning," she said, smiling as if this were any other day, as if she did this all the time. Her voice was almost normal, just slightly blurry. I felt like I was listening to a recording of her, with a faint static humming in the background.

I ignored the static. "Happy Thanksgiving!" I chirped, and practically skipped up next to her. If she was pretending to be happy, so would I.

"Here." She set a bag of apples and a peeler in front of me. "I'm making the pie."

I was about to ask about Dad's pie, but I swallowed the question. I didn't want to spoil the moment. The sight of her and the scent of freshly peeled apples made me want to leap up and wrap her in the biggest hug. But we were pretending this was normal, so I picked up an apple and started peeling.

The house rang with silence, but I didn't dare suggest music, so I listened to the song my peeler made. *Tsk, tsk, tsk.*

"Your father is picking Grandma up from the airport," she said. "She's looking forward to seeing us."

With all that's been happening, I hadn't even thought about my grandmother. She comes to our house every Thanksgiving, and Mom usually worries about her arrival for days in advance. Ever since her own parents died, these visits from her mother-in-law had taken on extra importance, and she'd putter around the house, cleaning and cooking, biting her nails as she went. This year, though, nothing worried her. Nothing seemed to affect her at all.

We cooked in silence for a while. "How's school?" Mom asked finally. She wasn't the type of mother who asked how school was. I normally just told her.

"Fine," I said. I wasn't the type of kid who said *fine.*

"How's the egg drop?"

Part of me couldn't believe she remembered. I thought back to our conversation in Dad's office, and it was almost like I'd been talking to a different person entirely. "It's going great!" My voice came out too loud.

"Did you try the cereal?"

"Yeah. It was great," I said, without really knowing why I'd lied.

Mom's smile didn't reach her eyes.

RECIPE FOR CRAN-APPLE PIE FILLING

MATERIALS:
- 5 green apples
- 1 cup cranberries
- ¾ cup white sugar
- 2½ tablespoons butter
- 1 teaspoon cinnamon
- ½ teaspoon nutmeg

PROCEDURE:
1. Preheat oven to 375 degrees.
2. Peel apples while Mom measures.
3. Do not put on Bon Jovi.
4. Just mix. Mix and pretend everything is as it should be.

Dad arrived with my grandmother, who started shedding layers as soon as she stepped into our overheated house. Off with the coat, the scarf, the leather gloves—all piled into Dad's arms.

"Oh, my big girl," she said, her accent thick, her hair dyed blacker than ever. "Look at you growing into a woman." Out of her knockoff Louis Vuitton purse came gifts from Korea—dried squid and colorful erasers and pajamas with dancing cartoon dogs and cats.

"Thanks, Grandma," I said, accepting the gifts and acting as if that weren't the most awkward thing to hear.

"I always tell you, call me *Halmoni,*"[18] she said as she hugged me, but she didn't really mean that by now. It was an old habit, our standard greeting.

Never in my whole life have I called her Halmoni. The first time I remember her saying that, Dad laughed this strange off-center laugh and said, "Okay, *Grandma.*" And that was it. She'd raised him on her own, and he said he'd had enough Korean words and foods and customs while growing up. He didn't want any more "culture" in his life, and he could go on forever pretending the Korean half of him didn't exist.

And then my grandmother was talking—about her recent trip to Korea and her archnemesis neighbor and

---

18 *Halmoni, n.:* the Korean word for "grandmother."

her forty-two-year-old boyfriend who she insists we call Uncle Gene. She splits her time between her family in Korea and Uncle Gene in California, and by the time she makes her way to us for Thanksgiving, she always has a treasure trove of tales. The way she was speaking reminded me of the way Mom used to be, even though they aren't related—bubbling up with laughter and stories, hands dancing in front of her.

We got to eating quickly—that's the way of my family—and if my grandmother felt uncomfortable with the white food, she didn't say anything.

When I was younger, she would come over and cook all of her—and my—Korean favorites, *bibimbap, kalbi, mandoo,* but Dad would never eat them. He winked at me and said, "I've eaten enough of Grandma's cooking for a lifetime." I've never thought about it before, how weird that was, how much he says without really saying. All I know is I will eat my mom's cran-apple pie forever.

And by the time that cran-apple pie did come around, Mom was smiling and eating and asking Grandma questions. I could almost forget about the "situation." I could almost forget about the quiet nights, quiet mornings, quiet, quiet darkness that had settled around our house for the past four months. I could almost forget about Dad bumping around the kitchen, navigating pots and pans he rarely used, and me stumbling through the science homework she'd always helped me with. Seeing her smile—seeing her eat and smile and laugh—I could almost forget all that.

Almost, but not quite.

After dinner, we sat in the living room, with Mom and Grandma and me on the couch. Grandma stroked my hair exactly the way Mom used to. Eventually, she made me change into my new pajamas, with the dancing cats and dogs, and I put them on for her, even though they were too scratchy and too small.

"Ipuda," Grandma gasped when she saw me.[19]

Dad stiffened at the Korean language. He always does that. I don't know why.

I laid my head on my grandmother's lap, and I felt like a little kid again, listening to my family talk around me. At one point, Dad started talking about his work, about his research, and I fell asleep to the sound of his voice.

Even as I slipped into sleep, I could feel Mom fading into the background, and Dad kept talking, and all the world was backward—but I couldn't quite remember how our family used to be.

• • •

---

[19] *Ipuda, adj.:* the Korean word for "beautiful." When I was little, my grandmother said it to me so many times that I thought it was my Korean name. I told people Ipuda was my Korean name, until Dad heard me saying it and told me to stop.

I woke up in my bed the next morning, disoriented and panicked, as if I'd had a nightmare. When I went downstairs, Dad was in the kitchen, taking plates out of the dishwasher and stacking them in their right cabinets—cleaning up and erasing all the evidence of last night. Grandma was staying at a hotel nearby, and we were all supposed to get brunch later—but Mom wasn't around. Their bedroom door was shut tight.

"Good morning, Natalie!" Dad said, his voice trying way too hard to be happy. He pointed to the top rack of the dishwasher. "Why don't you help put the glasses away?"

I walked over to him and started working on the glasses, and we stepped through the kitchen in silence, with nothing but the sound of clinking dishware. I couldn't wait to see Grandma again, because she would fill us with her noise—and she would bring Mom back again.

"Natalie," Dad said. His voice was still trying too hard. "Remember how we agreed on your appointment? I spoke with a therapist I think you'll really like. She's a friend—"

"Okay," I cut him off real quick. I picked up two more glasses, but they felt so heavy in my hands all of a sudden, and I set them down on the counter. Too hard. "Where's Mom?" I asked, because I couldn't hold my question any longer.

Dad frowned. "She's just in the bedroom, but—"

I tried to slip past him—I needed to see her, to make sure the happy, smiling Mom from last night wasn't just an illusion—but he stopped me.

"Don't wake her just yet," he said. There was an edge to his voice that I didn't want to think about. "She's sleeping." The word *sleeping* was layered with a thousand different meanings, and I was pretty sure I would never understand half of them, but I knew the most important one.

Mom has a note in her book, just a paragraph long, called "A Word on Words." She talks about all those pretty scientific words, all those Big Terms, and justifies all those footnotes in her book. She says how important it is to understand, to know the meaning of the words, because once you *know* a word, you can own it—it's yours, and it's a part of you.

I used to leaf through her book, reading only the footnotes, trying to memorize all those big definitions, trying to understand her indecipherable language. But some words are too big to be contained. Some words take on new, unexpected definitions that you can't find in the dictionary.

So when Dad said Mom's *sleeping,* the word swallowed me whole and spat me back out. I went up to my room and refused to go out for brunch. I read all the footnotes in Mom's book until my mind was filled only with plant words and all my worries stopped pounding in my head.

ASSIGNMENT 17: MAGNETS

QUESTION: How does temperature affect magnets?

MATERIALS:
- 3 magnets
- 1 hot plate
- 50 washers
- 1 beaker of ice water
- Tongs

HYPOTHESIS: Hot magnets work better than cold magnets.

Mondays are always hard, but on the Monday after Thanksgiving weekend you can tell nobody wants to be in school—not the kids, not the teachers, not the janitors or the lunch ladies. There's a sleepiness in everyone's eyes, a slowness in their steps, a sadness in their voices.

I was the only one happy to be in school, happy not to be home.

Twig came to science class dragging. "School is the worst torture in the world," she said, leaning her head against my shoulder as the rest of Fountain Middle's seventh graders slumped toward their desks.

"Good weekend?" I asked.

"I was with my dad, so yes."

Twig loves her dad more than she loves her mom— she always says so—but I don't know why. She only sees her dad a few times a year, and even though Twig's mom works a lot, she's always there for Twig, always trying. Sometimes Twig seems backward to me. We've been best friends for years now, but I don't always get her.

"What about you?" she asked.

"My grandmother came over." My stomach clenched as I thought of Grandma leaving this morning, taking her flurry of noise with her.

"Did she give you weird Japanese presents?"

"Korean, and yes."

"Any board games?"

97

"No, sorry."[20]

Twig sighed. "I guess I shouldn't have expected anything to make this day better."

Twig was always in a bad mood whenever she left her dad's house. That, at least, made sense to me. A few months ago, I couldn't imagine what that felt like, having a parent disappear on you. Now maybe I kind of could.

Mr. Neely clapped his hands to get us settled, and we made our way to our seats. Even he was in a somber mood today. Holidays, apparently, don't make people happy. They just remind us of what we're missing every other day of the year.

"Today we are starting our physical science unit, and we will begin with *magnets*!" Mr. Neely said, trying to be chipper as usual. "At your workstations, you will find six magnets, and you will expose these magnets to different thermal conditions. One magnet will be hot, one cold, and one at room temperature. Please work in groups of two or three."

I think he said some more stuff after that, going on about magnet facts and educated guesses, but I wasn't listening anymore. Twig and I were autopiloting over to our table in the back.

---

20 My grandmother did give me a Korean video game once. It had to do with both aliens and yoga and was surprisingly addictive, but Twig refused to play it. "It sounds awesome," she said, shaking her head sadly. "But I'm a purist."

"I miss Renaldo," Twig sighed.

"Renaldo?" I said as we settled onto our lab stools and started rearranging our materials.

"Our frog," she said, as if that were obvious.

I blinked at her. "You mean the one we dissected."

Twig held a hand up and looked to the sky. "Rest in peace."

Mr. Neely was instructing us to note our materials and hypotheses in our lab books, and I was vaguely listening, and vaguely following instructions, when Dari pulled up a stool and sat down at our table. He didn't even say anything—just sat down.

Here's a hypothesis: Twig wouldn't take kindly to a newcomer.

"Um," I said.

Twig narrowed her eyes at him in a way that was meant to be intimidating, but kind of made her look like a sleepy cat. I realized I'd never told her about Dari's potato and our weird mini-conversation, although I'd meant to.

"George is sick," Dari said, referring to his usual lab partner. Dari seemed older than everyone else in our year, not in the way he looked—although he was the tallest boy in our class—but in the way he *was*. He didn't seem to care when people looked at him funny, and he didn't react the way Twig did, by doing something even *weirder*. He just shrugged and smiled and kept looking you right in the eye. It made me uncomfortable.

Other people started looking at him weird, too, and Mikayla whispered something to Janie. I knew she was probably surprised Twig and I were talking to a boy, and she was probably saying something mean about us, but I almost didn't blame her.[21] If George was sick, Dari should've gone with Tom K. and Nick, because boys went with boys and girls went with girls. That's pretty much the unspoken rule of middle school.

Dari shrugged and smiled and continued to sit next to us.

When it became obvious that he wasn't moving, Twig grunted and slid our materials over to him. "Might as well get started."

So Dari got started. We watched him scribble notes into his lab book and organize the materials, and within five minutes, we had a hot magnet, a cold magnet, and a magnet at room temperature.

"Sorry, I should've let you guys help more. I guess I got kind of carried away." His cheeks got darker, and he seemed genuinely sorry for doing all the work. "George doesn't really contribute at all, so . . ."

Twig gaped at the magnets. Her mouth actually fell

---

21 Okay, I mean, I guess I kind of do blame Mikayla. Boys are part of the reason we aren't friends anymore, after all. In fourth grade, she became obsessed with boys and wanted to pretend we all had boyfriends and discuss which one of us would get a boyfriend first, and who even cares?

open. Normally, it takes us the whole class period to do an experiment because we get distracted talking about which superpower we'd rather have[22] and then realize halfway through that we never listened to the directions and did the project entirely wrong.

"Well." Twig nodded, her face serious. "We *would* have liked to contribute more, but if you let me do the hot magnet, I won't tell on you."

Dari smiled big and stuck out his hand for Twig to shake. Then he stuck his hand out for me, and as we shook on it, I could tell he *got* us.

Maybe we kind of got him, too.

Twig picked up the tongs and plucked a magnet off the hot plate. It took her a couple tries to get it, but once she did, she yelped in excitement and held the magnet over the washers. We counted how many washers the hot magnet picked up, a grand total of thirteen. Dari did room temperature and got twenty-one. I did cold and got twenty-nine.

Twig jumped up and shouted, "You won, Natalie! You won!"

I smiled at Twig, but I felt a twisting in my stomach— like my hypothesis was wrong and the world didn't work quite like I thought it did.

Then Dari started explaining *why* the cold magnet

---

22 Me: invisibility. Twig: shape-shifting.

worked best—something about hot magnets having disorderly molecules—and Twig nodded along like she was actually listening. She was being so un-Twig-like, paying attention to our science experiment, so I tuned them out and started doodling snowflakes and flowers in my notebook.

It's funny how the cold magnets actually worked best. It's like how perennial plants seem to die in the winter, but really, they're just waiting till everything is all right again. Maybe it's not such a surprise that there's strength in the cold. Maybe sometimes the strongest thing of all is knowing that one day you'll be all right again, and waiting and waiting until you can come out into the sun.

After school, as Twig and I were biking back to her house, bundled up against the too-cold air, she said, "I think we should adopt him."

For one strange moment, I thought she was talking again about Renaldo, our cut-open frog, but then she said, "We'd never have to struggle through those assignments, and we'd get A's just for sitting there."

All at once, she was the Twig I knew and the Twig I did not know. She was the smart girl who schemed to get out of schoolwork, but also a stranger who suggested hanging out with someone new. She hadn't done that in all the years I'd known her.[23]

I shrugged. "That'd be great, but Dari was only sitting with us because George was out sick."

Twig frowned and pedaled faster, so we were no longer side by side. "Easy come, easy go!" she shouted into the crackling autumn air.

---

[23] One time when I slept over at Twig's place, her mom commented that Twig should try to branch out and find more friends than just me. This was a little insulting, to be honest, but Twig shut her down real fast. "I don't need anyone else, thank you very much," she said. Clarissa never brought it up again—at least not in front of me—and I never asked about it, either.

DECEMBER 1

ASSIGNMENT 18:
COUNTING ~~ON MOM~~ TO 100

Is it possible to be mad at someone for being sad?

When I got home tonight, Mom was sitting on the couch, watching some cooking show on TV, and I sat down next to her and started telling her about the whole magnet-Dari weirdness from earlier this week—about how Twig actually suggested hanging out with someone new. About how she said it was just to get A's, but they got along really well, and she seemed to like being around Dari. I wasn't sure what to make of this new Twig—I wasn't even sure why I was so upset—and I needed a mom. I needed someone to help sort all of this out.

Mom smiled and nodded along, but I could tell she wasn't really listening. I know she was trying, and I know Dad says this blankness isn't her fault, but none of that mattered to me anymore because I was sitting right in front of her and she wasn't listening.

"Twig and I were working on the egg drop project," I said, thinking maybe, when it came to science, she might pay attention. "But the eggs kept breaking. We probably need help."

Mom stared off into space before turning toward me, as if she were in slow motion. "Sorry, honey. What was that?"

Looking into her eyes was like peering over the edge of a well and not being able to see the bottom. I wanted to shake her. I wanted to jump on the couch and wave my arms in the air and scream.

But I turned away from her bottomless eyes. "Nothing," I said, before walking out of the living room and into my bedroom.

She didn't try to stop me.

I shut my door—quietly, because I couldn't quite bring myself to slam it—and I lay down on my bed. I tried to count to one hundred. Back when I was little and used to throw temper tantrums, Dad would walk me to my room, sit me on my bed, and tell me to count to one hundred. Once I finished, everything would be okay again.

One.

Two.

Three.

The thing is: Mom was laughing on Thanksgiving. She did it for Grandma. *That's* trying. But she doesn't care enough to try for me. In the back of my mind, I thought about my winter sickness, about all those days she spent in bed with me, comforting me, refusing to leave me, but I buried those thoughts and counted.

When I got to fifty-two, I made a resolution: if she doesn't care about me, I'm not going to care about her. She is not my mom right now. She is an impostor in my mother's skin.

I hate her.

I hate her.

I hate her.

ASSIGNMENT 19: 2 + 1, AKA NOT-SO-ADVANCED ALGEBRA

Twig got in trouble today. This should not be surprising, given the Eyewash Incident and the Stolen Turtle Incident,[24] but it's still annoying. Twig is a person who doesn't know when to stop. To her, the word *no* is a challenge, and I get why she drives teachers nuts. Sometimes I want to shake her and say, *TWIG, STOP.* But of course that would only make her do whatever she's doing louder.

Anyway, she snuck into the teachers' lounge during lunch and drank half a pot of cold coffee, just because she's not allowed to drink it and she was curious. Basically, she went wild. Like, Twig $\times$ 1,000. She wouldn't stop talking

---

[24] Again, don't ask.

or bouncing around in class. So, of course, she had to have a "talking-to" from our principal—which is probably the hundredth talking-to Twig has had at this school. She told me I didn't have to wait for her after school, but I said I would anyway. I didn't feel like going home yet.

Dari was sitting by the lockers again. Of course he was. Since Dari's last name starts with a *K,* his locker is in the exact middle of the hallway—halfway between Twig's and my lockers.

"I thought only losers stayed after school," he said as I hovered in front of Twig's locker.

"I don't think I said *losers,*" I replied.

He laughed. "So why are you hanging around?"

I walked over to him, because it was kind of awkward having a conversation with fifteen lockers between us. "Twig's in trouble. Well, not trouble-trouble—her parents donate so much to the school that she never really gets in trouble for stuff." I think that might have been an over-share.

He smiled but didn't respond. Dari doesn't say much—he's a thinker. And it's like he needs to have all his words stored up and ready to go before he speaks.

"Advanced algebra again?" I asked, pointing to the book in his lap.

He shook his head and turned his lab notebook for me to see.

"Oh," I said, moving closer to look at the diagrams he'd

been drawing. "That's for the egg drop contest." I wasn't sure why I was surprised. Of course he was entering the contest. Mr. Neely had mentioned something about Dari and all the best, brightest students being involved.

He nodded. "I'm investigating acute angles and their effect on impact. Mr. Neely said I could use it for my scientific process project."

"Right," I said, as if he weren't speaking gibberish to me. "I'm doing it, too."

His grin widened, and I immediately regretted telling him. He was my competition, which probably made him my sworn enemy or something. I don't know. I don't really do competitions. He scooted over on the floor, even though there was plenty of space, so I assumed that was a signal for me to sit. I sat.

"Have you come up with a design yet?" he asked.

"Um."

"You don't have to tell me if you don't want to." He was talking quickly and blushing again. "I didn't mean to pry."

Mom would've shaken her head at that. *A scientist never apologizes for asking questions,* she'd say. *Questions keep us alive.*

"No, it's okay. We've come up with designs. They just haven't exactly worked out."

He smiled. "If you wanted, we could team up?"

I hesitated, thinking about splitting the money three

ways, instead of just two. And then I remembered the magnet project. And also all the eggs Twig and I had broken. "Why? I'm sure you can do it on your own."

He shrugged, matter-of-fact. "I probably can."

I was trying to figure out what to say to that when Twig popped out of the stairwell and made her way over, bouncing on her Sharpied-up Converse. The seventh-grade classrooms are on the top floor of the school, and we all hate those stairs, but Twig never seems winded by the three-story climb.[25]

She glanced between Dari and me and gave me a weird look. "Hi."

I stood up quickly, feeling guilty without knowing why. "Twig! How'd it go?"

She rolled her eyes. "Principal Nutter Butter[26] thought it would be a good idea for me to learn respect, maybe see a counselor, the usual."

See a counselor. I thought about Dad and my stomach clenched. "Twig," I said, "Dari offered to team up with us on the egg project."

"Us?" Dari asked, looking between Twig and me. He

---

25 The eighth graders have the second floor, and the sixth graders have the first floor. Supposedly, the third floor is better than the first, because we don't have to be by the cafegymnasitorium, but I don't exactly buy that. I think the teachers just didn't want to scare the brand-new sixth graders into switching schools.

26 Technically, it's Principal Nutt-Burter—can you really blame us for the nickname?

was grinning like this was the best news ever. The kid was weird.

"*Us,*" Twig said, gesturing between me and her and making her wannabe-intimidating sleepy-cat face.

"Twig and I are working together," I explained, even though I think he'd already figured that out.

"Great." Dari smiled like he meant it.

Twig adjusted the straps of her backpack. "We have to go," she informed him—and me—and walked off without another word, her footsteps echoing, pounding down the stairs.

I gave Dari an awkward wave before running after her. "Are you okay?" I asked once we made it to the first floor.

"What is it—am I not smart enough for you? Am I not a good enough partner anymore?" she asked. She walked out of the school and wouldn't slow down.

"*He* volunteered himself," I said. "I didn't have anything to do with it. And I figured it couldn't hurt. You're the one who said we should team up with him more often!"

"Yeah, for class."

"This *is* for class. Basically." I couldn't make sense of her. One second she wanted to work with Dari, and the next she didn't.

"Except we're doing it for fun, too. Together."

We'd gotten to our bikes by then, and Twig swung her

leg over the seat, hovering with her tiptoes touching the ground. I unlocked my bike. "If he helps us, we'll get A's on our project. And we'll probably win the money."

"Who cares about money?" Twig asked.

Like I said, sometimes Twig and I are from totally different galaxies. "*I* care. And it'll still be fun. I promise."

Twig sighed up a windstorm, keeping her eyes on her bike. "Fine, fine. He can join us. I gotta get home now. My mom is having some supermodel friends over." She pushed her feet against the pedals and left me behind. I couldn't tell if she was lying, but either way, I wasn't invited.

Either way, I'd have to go home eventually.

When I got home, Mom was in her room with the door shut, so I did the same. I went straight past Dad without saying a word and went into my bedroom and locked the door. Mom's book was still lying on my bed, and I threw it across the room. It hit the wall and landed on the floor facedown, spine bent open, the pages crumpled beneath it. I told myself I didn't care, that I never wanted to read a word of that book again, but five minutes later I was on the floor smoothing out the pages, reading those paragraphs for the thousandth time, repeating the Latin words like a secret spell.

Orchidaceae. *Cattleya. Fortis.*

ASSIGNMENT 20: DUE NORTH

It didn't take long for Mr. Neely to get his enthusiasm back. Today in class he announced we'd continue working with magnets—apparently otherwise known as "natural magic!" Seriously, I have no idea where Mr. Neely finds all his excitement, but I wish I could siphon some of it off and give it to Mom.

Anyway, when we broke into groups to make compasses, Dari came over to sit with Twig and me. George was back in school today, but he joined Tom K. and Nick without hesitation, as if that was the way it had always been. Nobody else in class seemed to even notice the switch-up—except for Mikayla, that is, who stared at us from across the room, frowning.

I expected Twig to make a scene, like she had a few days ago, but she took a deep breath and stayed silent. Dari raised an eyebrow at her, and she shrugged, and some kind of communication passed between them that I couldn't catch. Then he sat down and began writing:

MATERIALS:
- Needle
- Magnet
- Wax paper
- Bowl
- Water

Dari finished our compass quickly and accurately, as expected, and Twig grinned in approval as she copied his notes into her lab book. She leaned in close to him, her long blond hair forming a curtain between me and Dari's book,[27] so I just played with a couple of leftover magnets, flipping one over so it attracted all the other magnets on the table, and then turning it so it repelled everything in its path, like, *No thanks, not for me.*

"We need a plan of action for this egg drop competition," Dari said once they'd finished with the lab, and I startled at his voice, at the sound of reality.

---

[27] Technically, we're supposed to tie our hair up for every lab, but Twig rarely does. I don't think she has since we cut up Renaldo, and that was only because she didn't want to get frog guts in her hair.

"Aye, aye, Captain," Twig said, all sarcastic. I knew she was still upset from the other day, but I don't think Dari could tell.

He frowned. "I don't think I should be the captain here."

Twig put her pencil to her lips and said, very seriously, "You're right. You're too much of a nerd."

Dari considered this. "Can I be mission analyst instead? I like analyzing."

Twig squinted at him, and I worried she was going to say something mean, but she said, "You can be mission analyst as long as I'm head sheriff. That means what I say goes, and if you mess up, you're out."

Instead of getting offended or weirded out like most people would have, Dari said, "Pleased to make your acquaintance, Head Sheriff," and laughed and shook her hand. These were things Dari did a lot—laugh and shake hands.

"Well, okay," I said. I wanted to change the subject. I didn't like the way they were looking at me—as if they were waiting for an answer on a test I hadn't studied for. "But let's focus less on these nicknames and more on our egg designs." My voice sounded cactus-prickly compared to their light, joking tones—and for a wild second, I worried all the fun had drained out of me.

Twig looked at me and raised her eyebrows, then

glanced at Dari. All of a sudden, they were a team, and I wasn't sure if I liked it. He did all the work and joked around with her—and maybe she'd replace me. But she smiled. "I think we've found our captain."

Dari laughed and raised his hand to me in salute. Twig did the same.

And I did not cry—because it's way embarrassing to cry in the middle of your science classroom. But still, it was pretty nice. Our compass-ized needle floated in our bowl of water on its little wax paper raft, pointing north, at me.

"I'm not sure I know how to be a captain," I said, wishing my voice sounded less serious. They were making this a game, and I was making it weird.

But Dari grinned, and Twig laughed. "Of course you do," she said, before flicking the compass needle and spinning it round and round.

Aye aye, Captain!
Head Sheriff reporting for duty.
First order of business:
Our Mission Analyst is a NERD!

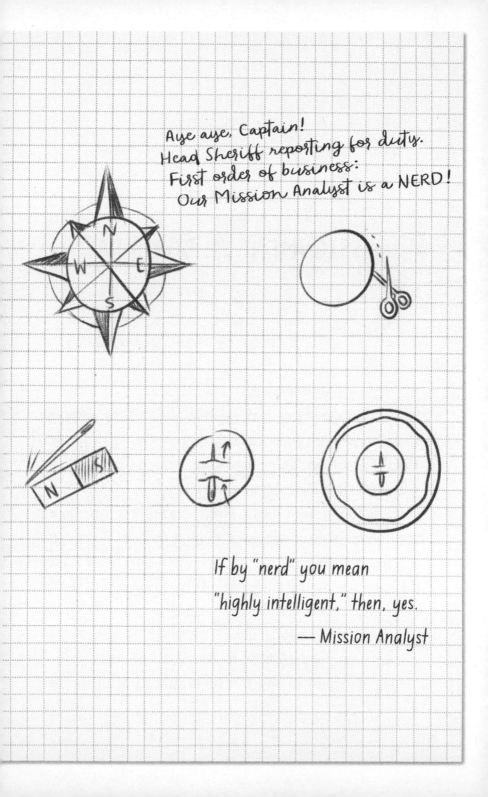

If by "nerd" you mean

"highly intelligent," then, yes.

— Mission Analyst

ASSIGNMENT 21: DORIS DAY

Well, I guess Dad finally decided to stop "giving me some space" and start enacting a *plan of action,* shall we say. He picked me up from school today, which was sign number one that something was Not Okay.

"I'm biking home with Twig," I said. I felt stubborn about it all of a sudden, even though I'd been dreading it all day. The weather had cracked, the temperature finally dropping below freezing. We all had our down jackets out today, finally admitting to ourselves that winter was a thing that was happening.

"You can put your bike in the trunk," he said.

This is weird to say, but seeing Dad out in the real

world was unsettling. I hadn't realized until then how sucked up we'd been in Mom's sadness. The two of us were compass needles, pointing straight at Mom. We hadn't done anything outside together in months. I think Dad was realizing it, too, because when I got into the passenger seat, he wrapped an arm around me and pulled me into an awkward hug.

"This will be good," he said. "Doris is really good." Which was sign number two, because anything involving someone named Doris is definitely Not Okay.[28] I didn't ask who Doris was, partly because I didn't want to know, and partly because I already did know.

My palms started to sweat.

Dad tried to make small talk on the whole drive over, even though he's not very good at small talk. The drive took us in the same direction as Lancaster University, where Mom used to work. We had to go through a rundown part of town, and as we drove past those buildings, I wrapped my jacket tighter around my chest, even though Dad was blasting the heater. Thinking about going back to Mom's lab made me feel kind of sick inside, like even just the thought of it was somehow a betrayal.

---

[28] Is it just me, or does the name Doris automatically make you think of a lunch lady? Or an old woman who knits cat sweaters? Sorry if your name is Doris—just, you know.

But once we made it through the beat-up neighborhood, we turned left instead of right, and we kept on driving. Eventually, we made it to the parking lot of an unfriendly concrete office building. I was so upset by that point that I wanted to grab my bike out of the trunk and pedal all the way home. Only I didn't know how to get back, and it was really far, and anyway, Dad would have been really angry if I did that, so I followed him into the building and into Dr. Doris McKenna's lobby.

Taking me to a therapist's office without telling me was basically an act of guerrilla warfare,[29] and I promised myself right then that I'm never going to do this ambush stuff to my kids. I'm never gonna act like I know best and they aren't capable of making their own decisions.

I'm pretty sure I had cartoon steam coming out of my ears, because Dad knew I was fuming and didn't even try to make small talk anymore. We sat in the waiting room, and he picked up one of those doctor's office *National Geographic*s, propping one ankle over his knee and reading as if everything was cotton-candy-dandy.

I crossed my arms over my chest, and Dad looked up and frowned. He had the nerve to look confused. "Natalie?"

---

[29] Guerrilla warfare, *n.*: We learned about guerrilla warfare and its ambush strategy in school last year, and of course everyone started making jokes about *gorilla warfare,* and all the boys spent the whole lunch period jumping around and scratching their heads and armpits and grunting like gorillas because middle school boys are the most embarrassing creatures on the face of the planet.

I glared at him.

He rubbed his hand over the side of his face, looking all concerned, like he just realized he made a mistake. "Natalie, we talked about this. Your appointment—remember?"

I mean, I know he'd mentioned the appointment before, but I never really thought it would happen. And it still didn't feel fair. He'd made this decision for me—I didn't want to be there.

I looked around. The waiting room was too small and about a million degrees too hot. And I was planning my great escape when the therapist's door opened.

Dr. Doris came out to call my name. She was young and pretty, with horn-rimmed glasses and red hair, and she had this huge smile when she said my name, but I just glared at her. I felt kind of bad because the woman was only doing her job, and anyway *she* hadn't forced me to come here, so she didn't really deserve my scowl face.

But then Dad gave a thumbs-up and said, "Good luck, Nats," and I didn't feel bad for scowling anymore.

Dr. Doris's office is different from Dad's office. Dad's office is painted this creamy white color, and all his furniture is white, but her office is colorful. Everything is bright: bright peach walls, bright blue furniture, bright sunlight streaming in through big bright windows. Colorful little toys sit on her coffee table—Rubik's Cubes and Slinkys—and her windows are lined with about twenty different plants, with all different-colored flowers, and I have to admit the whole happy-garden feel of the place made me more comfortable. Only then I worried this was some kind of Therapist Trick to *make* me more comfortable, and then I had no idea how to feel.

"It's so lovely to meet you, Natalie. I've heard so many great things about you," Dr. Doris said. Which meant Dad had already talked to her about me. Which was definitely Not Okay. But whatever. "I'm Dr. Doris McKenna, but you can call me Doris."

Her smile was kind and inviting, but I knew a Therapist Trick when I saw one. I wasn't about to call her Doris, as if we were friends—as if I actually *wanted* to talk to her, instead of being forced here against my will.

I half shrugged in response.

"How have you been feeling lately?" she asked.

I didn't want to answer, but I'd already been pretty rude, so I said, "Fine," because that was better than saying nothing at all.

Dr. Doris smiled and nodded as if she was waiting for me to continue, so I said, "I don't want to talk about my mom."

The look she gave me was so sympathetic and understanding that I almost started crying right there. I was surrounded by tissue boxes that seemed to be demanding, *Cry! Cry already!* But I did not.

"What *do* you want to talk about, Natalie?"

I hated the way she said my name, all intimately as if we were best friends.[30]

"I'm working on a project for school," I said, because adults love when you talk about school.

Dr. Doris's smile got extra big, and I could tell I was right because, even though she was trained specifically to talk to kids, she was still an adult, so she fell for the whole *look, I'm taking initiative in school* thing. "And what is this project?" she asked.

So I told her about Operation Egg and the scientific process and Dari and Twig and all that business. I did *not* tell her about the five hundred dollars or my secret plan for that money.

"Twig and Dari said I should be the team captain," I added, and immediately regretted mentioning it. I'd given her something to latch onto. I burrowed the toe of my sneaker into the teal-blue rug as if I could drill a hole right through the ground.

Dr. Doris tilted her head. "How do you feel about being the team captain?"

Which—ugh. It sounded like a question Dad would ask. I shrugged. "Fine, I guess."

---

[30] Twig, my *real* best friend, hardly ever says my name. She just says, *Hey, you,* and I'm expected to know she's talking to me, because who else would she be talking to?

Dr. Doris set her notebook on the end table next to her and leaned forward. "You look like you might be a little nervous, which would be perfectly understandable."

It was like, since she couldn't talk about Mom Problems, she had to go poking around to find another problem, but everything was totally fine. I mean, of course I was a little nervous. Every time I thought about the competition, I got that plum-pit feeling in my stomach, and being the captain made it even scarier—*lonelier*, too.

But I wasn't about to tell her any of that.

I looked at my shoes and shrugged.

When Dr. Doris spoke, her voice was softer. "Have you talked to your parents about the egg project?"

"Operation Egg," I corrected.

"Right."

"Yeah, I have."

And I'll spare you all the boring details, because the conversation pretty much went that way for the next hour. Dr. Doris kept steering our conversation toward my parents, and I kept steering it away, so we talked a whole lot about nothing.

I looked at the clock and counted down—fifty minutes, forty minutes, twenty, ten—and in the home stretch, at five minutes left, she said, "I know you weren't ready to talk about your mom today, and I respect that, but next week I'd like to discuss the situation a little further."

I couldn't have said anything but *Okay,* so that was what I said.

When I came out, Dad didn't even ask me how it went, but he gave me a hug, which was embarrassing. Happiness and relief practically radiated off him. As much as I love my dad and know he's trying his best, when I came out of that office, I wanted to punish him. I pushed his hug away without saying anything, and I was quiet the whole ride home. When we pulled into the driveway, I got out and slammed the door, and I could feel his happiness shattering.

It's like I couldn't even help myself. Like suddenly I'm this terrible person who hurts her dad on purpose, and I don't even know why.

Maybe I could talk to Dr. Doris about that next week. Maybe not.

STEP 6: EXPERIMENT

And now for the moment you've all been waiting for!
Time to test those hypotheses! Will your educated
guesses stand up against the Great Scientific
Process?
#MomentOfTruth #GetPumped

ASSIGNMENT 22: THE FIRST TEST

Most of Twig's egg drop designs ended up being impossible to create, which was pretty unsurprising, but she insisted on making as many as she could and testing those out. Dari, Twig, and I stayed late after school yesterday, gluing and rearranging and cracking a whole bunch of eggs. Finally, we ended up with six designs, which was pretty impressive, if you ask me.

"I'm not sure if these are going to work," Dari said as we put the finishing touches on S'meggs, sticking random twigs into jumbo-size marshmallows. Basically, S'meggs was an egg attached to jumbo marshmallows and sticks and even bars of chocolate. It was inspired by a giant s'more, and I'm pretty sure Twig was hungry when she thought it up.

"The twigs keep breaking," Dari said as one of the twigs snapped.

Twig glared at him with that sleepy-cat face, as if that was a personal insult, and he didn't comment again.

We spent hours putting together our contraptions and didn't get home until late last night, but I insisted we get back to school bright and early this morning—despite it being a Saturday. We came up with a plan, and I have to admit, I was kind of excited.

Step 1: Observe. We have only a month until the egg drop competition—less, if you consider the holidays—so we need to get going with testing our eggs.

Step 2: Question. When can we test our egg designs by dropping them out of a third-story window?

Step 3: Investigative Research. Mikayla and the rest of the JV girls' volleyball team had their annoying spirit week these past few days, so we knew there'd be a volleyball game at Fountain Middle on Saturday. I double-checked their schedule online. The school would be open then, which meant we could easily get in and sneak up to the third-floor classrooms.[31]

Step 4: Hypothesis. Of course, I'm Managing My Expectations, but I'm sure at least a couple of our six egg drop designs will survive the fall. We'll probably have to decide which egg contraption is best.

Step 5: Procedure:

1. Twig sleeps over on Friday, and Dad drops us off at school in the morning so we can "go to the game and show school spirit," etc., etc.
2. Meet Dari at the school, and wait until the game starts and everyone is distracted. Then we pretend we need to use the bathroom, and we leave the cafegymnasitorium.[32]
3. Sneak up to the third floor, into Mr. Neely's classroom.

---

[31] Originally, we planned to ask Mr. Neely if we could use his window after school on Monday, but Twig shook her head and said sagely, "Better to ask forgiveness than permission." Dari cleared his throat and looked uncomfortable, but we decided to go with the Saturday plan, just in case.

[32] Cafeteria. Gymnasium. Auditorium. Except, you know, all in one.

4. Drop the eggs from the window.
5. Sneak back downstairs to examine the eggs and see which ones survived.
6. Clean up and escape before the game ends, without anybody noticing.

If anybody had told me just a couple months ago that I'd want to be at school at 8:00 a.m. on a Saturday, I would have laughed and called them Mr. Neely–level ridiculous, but I guess nothing this year was turning out how I'd expected.

Families wearing red-and-blue school colors were filing into the first-floor gym, and Twig and I dropped into the crowd with them. We were both wearing red-and-blue sweaters to blend in, but of course Twig had taken the "blending in" a step too far—so she was just standing out. She wore one red glove and one blue glove, and had written *Go!* on one cheek and *Red Pandas!* on the other cheek, in support of our mascot.[33] The *Red Pandas!* part was way too long, though, and she'd written the *d-a-s!* sideways down her jaw.

So basically, our school spirit disguises weren't great.

We followed the crowd into the school, hanging back

---

[33] Technically, we're the Fountain Middle Foxes—but the mascot costume definitely looks like a red panda. Most of us just shrug and let it go, but of course Twig needs to make a point about it.

The Plan

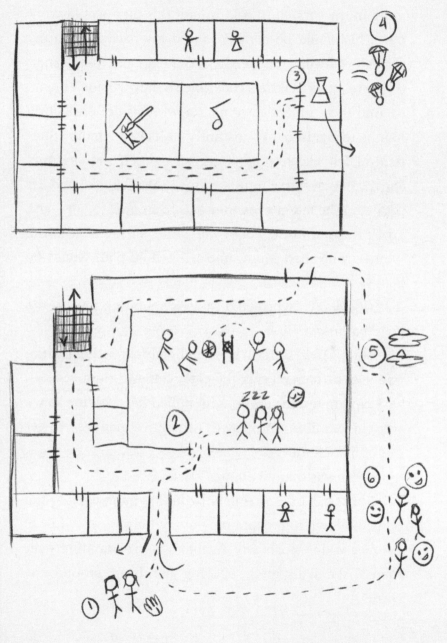

so nobody would spot us. I could hear my heart drumming in my ears, but I told myself this plan would work out. This would be okay. I shifted my backpack on my shoulders, feeling the weight of our eggs and their armor, trying to move as little as possible so they wouldn't break.

And then, up ahead of us, I saw a flash of dark curly hair. I recognized her instantly—Mikayla's mom. Suddenly I felt like I couldn't see straight. If she saw me, she'd come over, try to talk to me. She'd be fake and act nice, and she might even invite us to sit next to her—and I'd be trapped in the volleyball game, sitting next to the woman who fired Mom, and the whole plan would be ruined.

"This way," I whispered to Twig, pointing toward the girls' bathroom.

"But—" Twig started, but I'd already slipped out of the line, just before entering the cafegymnasitorium.

I ran around the corner and pulled her with me so we were hidden from the crowd. I think we managed to get out of line unnoticed.

"What was that all about?" Twig asked.

"I just . . ." I didn't finish. I couldn't quite explain the panic I felt without explaining everything.

Twig didn't push any further. "Dari's standing over there," she whispered, peeking her head around the corner.

I craned my neck to see, and there he was, standing in the middle of the hallway as the crowd passed him by, looking around and rocking back and forth on his heels. He fiddled with the hem of his T-shirt—which was not red and blue—and he looked so nervous that he might as well have worn a sign that said, *I'm about to break the rules!*

"Should I go get him?" Twig asked.

"Maybe you should wait until the game starts," I said, but Twig had run off before I'd even finished the sentence.

She grabbed him by the wrist and pulled him back toward me. A few people gave them strange looks but kept walking into the gym.

"Do you think anyone saw us?" Twig whispered loudly. Her hair was all staticky from the invisible electric current that seemed to run inside her. "Probably not, right? We were as stealthy as secret agent spies."

"Sure, Twig," I said.

Dari seemed so nervous and Twig was so confident that I couldn't help but laugh at how opposite they were.

Twig grinned back at me.

Inside the gym, a buzzer sounded, the crowd quieted, and we heard the squeak of sneakers that meant the game had begun.

"Ready?" I said.

They nodded, and I led them to the stairwell. We tip-toed up the steps, hearts beating in our ears, and when we got to the second-floor stairwell, we peeked down the hall, searching for teachers or an army of security guards. Of course there weren't any. This was just a JV volleyball game, after all.

We reached the third floor, and Dari and I held back as Twig ran ahead to be our lookout. She did somersaults and darted back and forth in zigzags, as if she were dodging laser beams. This all seemed like a game to Twig, a strategic board game come to life, and I was torn between telling her to take this seriously and joining in.

From across the hall, Twig said, "Do you think anyone knows we're here?" Her voice echoed.

Dari held a finger up for silence, trying not to laugh, and I could tell he felt as torn as I did.

Dari and I walked up to Mr. Neely's classroom door, and when Dari leaned forward, ready to turn the knob, Twig threw an arm out in front of him.

"Fingerprints," she hissed, before grabbing the knob with her own gloved hand.

The door didn't budge.

Twig looked over at me and bit her lip. I nudged her aside, not caring about fingerprints. The knob wouldn't turn. The door was locked. Which meant everything was officially *not* going according to plan.

"I think I can kick the door down," Twig suggested.

Dari put a hand on her shoulder. Then he turned red and took his hand off her shoulder. "Um, no. Don't kick the door." He shook his head. "I should have known the classrooms would be locked. I didn't consider it." Like he was the one who'd planned the whole thing, without any help at all.

"We'll have to wait until Monday," he said, nodding once, as if the decision had been made and there was nothing to do about it.

The logical, scientific part of my brain agreed with Dari. Of course we could wait until Monday. Of course Mr. Neely would let us test the design from his classroom window after school.

But, then again, we had the eggs, and we were here, and nothing was going according to plan. And maybe we *wouldn't* be allowed to drop the eggs on Monday. Maybe we wouldn't be able to test the eggs at all.

And then we wouldn't win the competition. And—

Twig took one look at my face and shook her head. "No," she said. "I have an idea. I think there's another way."

Twig led us down the hallway and walked into the girls' bathroom. "Come on," she said, sticking her head back out when we didn't immediately follow.

I glanced at Dari.

"Um," he said.

Twig rolled her eyes. "Oh, come on. Nobody's in here."

"But—"

"See, look," Twig said, and then she turned back to the bathroom and shouted, "Hello? Hello, anybody in here?"

"Twig," I hissed. "Quiet."

Dari still hesitated, and Twig threw her arms in the air, exasperated. "Don't be such a worrywart."

So we both followed her into the girls' bathroom, and Dari's face turned dark red. He kept his eyes glued to the floor.

"All right," Twig said, walking to the window by the sinks and tiptoeing to push it open. It was higher up and much smaller than the classroom windows, but we'd still be able to drop our eggs out of it.

I tiptoed and tried to see outside. "Yeah, this could work." Relief bloomed inside me.

"Um, guys," Dari said. "This is just a bathroom."

Twig squinted at him as if something were seriously wrong with him. I mean, really. He's supposed to be the smart one. "Yeah, Dari," she said slowly. "It is."

"No, but, I mean . . ." He cleared his throat and looked around, then looked at the ground, and then looked around again like he couldn't help it. "You guys don't have couches."

I blinked at him. "Does *your* bathroom have couches?"

"No, no, the boys' bathroom doesn't. It's just that all the guys say . . ."

We stared at him.

"Never mind," he said.

"Anyway," I said after a few seconds of awkward silence. I pulled my backpack off and carefully took out each egg contraption. Thankfully, they were all still intact. "We'll drop all six of these eggs. It would've been better to use Mr. Neely's windows, obviously, because we could've spread the eggs apart, but we'll just drop them on top of one another. I guess that'll be fine."

Dari cleared his throat, and Twig sighed, partly annoyed and partly amused. "What, Dari?"

I'd never seen him look so out of his element. He started tugging at the hem of his shirt again as if he were trying to drag himself down through the earth and disappear. It dawned on me then that if anybody caught us right now, he'd be in the most trouble.

"Dari," I said, "you can wait down by the crash site if you want."

His whole body relaxed. "Really?"

"Yeah. It makes more sense. You can move the old eggs out of the way and clear the space for the next drop."

He considered it, already inching toward the door. "That would be very helpful, actually. But I wouldn't want to leave you guys."

Twig stepped in, pulling a wad of paper towels and a plastic bag from the backpack and handing them to him. "It's okay, Dari. You can be the cleanup man. Plus, it's probably the most dangerous job of all—because if anyone catches you, you'll be standing there with a pile of eggs."

I hadn't considered that, and I worried it might be true, but Dari nodded, took the cleaning supplies, and ran out of the bathroom without another word.

As we waited for Dari to reach the bottom, Twig and I took each egg out of its protective wrapping and lined all of them up on the windowsill. They sat there in a row, ready to meet their fate.

To be honest, they looked pretty silly, and I wasn't quite sure how well they'd survive, but I couldn't think about that. I pushed all that doubt out of my head, and once Dari was ready for us, I picked up S'meggs, the s'mores-themed egg. The chocolate and marshmallows had melted slightly, so they stuck to my hands.

Twig raised her eyebrows. "The first drop. Should we make a speech?"

I laughed but avoided the question. I didn't want to make a big deal out of it. I didn't want to think too hard about what all this meant. I just wanted to drop the eggs and see which ones survived and get back to being okay.

"Be strong, little S'meggs," Twig said. "And fly safely."

I held it out the window. "Ready?"

Twig grinned. "Ready."

Down below, Dari stepped back and flashed a thumbs-up. I dropped S'meggs.

We couldn't see whether or not it survived. We just watched Dari sweep it aside to prepare for the next egg. Being up there, with the egg just a speck and the results unknown, was strange. I felt like anything was possible.

"That was awesome!" Twig said, slapping my back.

My hands were shaking, so I stuffed them into my pockets and let Twig pick up the next egg, which was covered in cotton balls: Cotton Ball Heaven.

"Dari's being weird," she said, peeking outside as she held the egg out, ready to drop it.

I leaned next to her and looked down at Dari, who was frantically waving his arms in the air.

She sighed and shook her head as if this were just some strange Dari quirk. "Ready?" she asked me.

"Twig, wait." I looked back down at Dari, who was now running around in a panic. "I think something's wr—"

A buzzer sounded downstairs, followed by the sounds of the big front doors opening and the chatter of parents.

I turned to Twig in horror. "The game! It must have been a blowout. Everyone's leaving now."

"Already?!" Twig stared back at me, frozen with her

arm still dangling out the window, fingers clamped around Cotton Ball Heaven.

"It's okay," I said, more to myself than to her. "It's okay. They're all going to exit through the front, and nobody has any reason to walk around behind the school. We just need to run down, clean up, and get out of here before anybody sees us."

Twig nodded. "Right, okay, let's go."

And then, without any word or warning, she swept her arm along the windowsill and pushed all the eggs out at once.

I gaped at my reckless, illogical best friend. Twig had done some inexplicable things over the past few years, but this was a whole new level. "Twig . . . why would you *do* that?"

She shook her head, eyes wide. "I had to destroy the evidence!"

"You didn't *destroy* evidence. You just splattered it all over!"

"I just—I don't know! I panicked!"

I didn't have time to deal with this. I grabbed Twig's wrist and we ran out of the bathroom.

"Abort mission! Abort!" Twig yelled wildly as we pounded down the three flights of stairs. I hissed at her to be quiet, and we rushed out the back doors to meet Dari.

"Oh *no*," Twig said when we reached him.

The Cotton Ball Heaven egg was smattered in his hair and sliding down the side of his face. On his forehead, just below his hairline, a red welt had started to form.

"All of the eggs broke," he informed us, holding out the remains. He'd haphazardly swept the remnants of the contraptions into the plastic bag, and yolk dripped from a hole at the bottom.

Neither Twig nor I knew exactly what to say, so we stood there for a second, looking at the bits of egg and cotton in his hair.

We needed to flee the scene of the crime, but it felt wrong to start running without acknowledging the obvious. "Are you okay?" I asked. I took the messy plastic bag from his hands.

Twig started picking eggshell out of his hair. "I hit you in the head. With an *egg*!"

At Twig's touch, the rest of Dari's face turned as red as the welt, and he cleared his throat. "Well," he said, his voice cracking. He cleared his throat again. "Well, the good news is that some of the eggs held up really well. *Much* better than expected. If you let me make some adjustments, I think I could make a couple of these work. The designs could actually make sense."

He braved a glance at Twig, who was still messing with his hair. "No offense."

Twig stepped back and shrugged, as if she hadn't created a totally awkward moment and then been insulted a second later. "Okay, Mission Analyst, we'll try it your way."

Even though the mission had totally and completely failed, their words made me hopeful. I let myself relax, feeling a little better, a little safer—until the back door opened and the girls' JV volleyball team streamed outside.

Mikayla and I locked eyes at the exact same time, and I saw her turn to Janie and say something before I quickly looked away.

"Um, we should probably go," I said to Twig and Dari, who were now *both* covered in yolk.

They looked up to see Mikayla walking over. Twig stuck out her jaw, like she always does when she's annoyed. Dari got this wide-eyed look of panic, as if Mikayla might tell a teacher what we'd done and get us in trouble.

There was no way she could know we'd been in the third-floor bathroom. At least, she couldn't *prove* that. But still, in that moment, I saw us through her eyes: A failed experiment. A mess. Totally hopeless.

Mikayla stopped in front of us and crossed her arms over her chest. "What are you doing?"

She was the tallest girl in our class, and she looked down at us like she was the queen of the world and we were her misbehaving subjects.

"None of your business," Twig said.

As weird as it is that Mikayla and I used to be friends, it's even weirder that *Twig* and Mikayla used to be friends. They're basically polar opposites, like magnets repelling each other.[34]

"We were just doing homework. For school," I said. It wasn't a lie, technically, but my heart beat loudly in my ears. I don't know why Mikayla makes me so nervous, and I hate that she does.

She looked like she was about to say something—probably something mean—but Janie ran up to Mikayla's side.

"What's going on?" Janie asked, looking confused. I realized that I didn't really know anything about Janie, except that she was friends with Mikayla. And she played volleyball.

"Nothing," Mikayla said, and then, just for good measure, she looked at me and added, *"Whatever,"* before turning and sashaying away with Janie.

"What is her *problem*?" Twig huffed.

Dari lifted a hand like he was going to comfort her, but ended up stuffing it into his pocket instead. "I'm sorry," he muttered.

We were all shaken up from the run-in with Mikayla, but Dari was seriously out of whack if he was apologizing

---

[34] See? Proof that I do pay attention in science class.

for being hit on the head. "It's not your fault," I said, which seemed like an obvious thing to say.

"Not about the eggs," he said. "I'm sorry because I should have stayed up there with you guys. I wasted so much time being indecisive and coming down here. I should have been part of the team."

I wasn't really sure why he was making such a big deal out of that, especially since it made sense for him to be down here anyway, but Twig just threw an arm around his shoulder, like a dad on some TV show. "No worries, Dari."

Dari looked down to hide his face, but not before I saw his goofy grin. Even covered in egg, he couldn't help but smile around her.

Twig, of course, was oblivious. "Next time we break into a girls' bathroom, you'll be right by our side," she said.

I really hoped she meant this metaphorically, not literally, but with Twig, it was a toss-up.

Dari laughed in an uncomfortable, strangled kind of way.

"Thank you, guys," I blurted. I didn't even care anymore about Mikayla or the failed mission. I had friends who were willing to get covered in yolk—and keep going anyway. "I just . . . thanks for being Team Egg."

Dari wiped yolk off his forehead and smiled. "Team Egg," he said, sticking his hand out, palm down.

I stared at him, not sure at first what he was doing, but Twig got it. She placed her hand on top of his and looked at me. "Come on, Natalie."

So I put my hand on theirs. All our hands were still covered in yolk, and somehow Twig's hand was also covered in glitter, although I don't remember including glitter in any of our contraptions.[35]

Dari counted down from three, and all at the same time, we said, "Team Egg!"

And it was so dorky and kind of embarrassing, and in the back of my mind I hoped Mikayla was already too far away to hear us, but none of that really mattered. Because these were my friends, and this was my team. And in that moment, I knew we had a chance.

---

[35] Twig's always doing this—adding "surprise glitter" to projects. She thinks it's hilarious, but anybody who's ever been in a second-grade classroom knows glitter is no joke. It's impossible to wash off.

ASSIGNMENT 23:
#MRNEELYSSNOWDAY

Twig, Dari, and I spent the rest of the weekend discussing our egg drop plans—except Wednesday, which is now officially Doris Day, unfortunately.

Dari started sketching out new diagrams and structures—building off Twig's wild ideas—and we made a plan to test the top two designs this weekend.

I'd hoped to spend all of science class today doodling up ideas for the new designs, and dreaming up travel plans for Mom and me—but Mr. Neely surprised us.

Because it's the last week of school before winter break, and because it snowed for the first time today, he decided to *actually* be the coolest teacher ever and let us skip class to play outside.[36]

We were supposed to be wrapping up our magnets-and-electricity unit, but really, there's not much more to learn about magnets after you've been talking about them for almost a month straight. Just to make sure everything was still "educational," he gave us a twenty-minute lecture about the science of snow before he set us free for the rest of the hour. (Cold temperatures, frozen water, ice, hail, snow, yes, yes, blah, blah.)

The weather was freezing, obviously, so we all pulled on our coats and scarves and bundled up up up, and Mikayla complained to infinity about how she would *literally* get frostbite, so Mr. Neely said anybody who didn't want to go outside was welcome to stay inside and finish an extra-fun science worksheet. He didn't even intend this as a punishment. He honestly thought it would be just as fun.

And that was how our whole seventh-grade science class ended up on the playground behind the school at the end of day on a Monday afternoon. At first nobody knew what to do, because we weren't exactly all friends, and we also weren't in second grade, so we weren't going to start spontaneously running around and playing tag.

---

36 Granted, he insisted on referring to this as #MrNeelysSnowDay, but still.

Also, Mr. Neely was standing there watching us, which was kind of weird.

Then Tom K. threw a snowball, because that's just the kind of kid he is.[37] The snowball flew fast and hit Nick Henner right in the face, and we all kind of held our breath because Nick used to be a big crybaby about that stuff, and who knew if he'd outgrown it?

But Nick started laughing, and he threw his own snowball, which hit George, and just like that, everyone was throwing snowballs. Even Mikayla and Janie threw some, before they went and sat on a bench to watch, because they don't like fun or something.

Twig tackled me into the snow, and I wriggled to get up, but she deadweighted on top of me until I said, "I give up, I give up!" Twig rolled off me, onto her back, and started making a snow angel, right in the middle of the snowball fight. And, of course, I started making one, too. This day was a beautiful good day in the middle of so many bad ones, and I felt like if I didn't laugh I would cry. And I don't even know what came over me—but I started laughing and laughing and I couldn't stop.

Dari ran over and hovered above us with an armload of snow.

---

37 Tom K. was also the kid who started the whole "gorilla warfare" business last year, just saying.

"No!" I shrieked, struggling to get up, but he dumped the snow over Twig and me before we could squirm away.

"Dari, you big nerd!" Twig yelled, but she said it nicely, if you can believe it. Dari's cheeks were flushed with the cold, but he was grinning so wide. It felt good to see him having fun instead of sitting outside classrooms doing homework.

Twig reached down and started throwing fistfuls of snow at Dari, because she couldn't be bothered to make snowballs. George threw a snowball, and it hit Dari in the back of the head, but he ignored it. He was too busy happy-awkward-nervous-laughing and looking at Twig. And then he took off in a sprint, and Twig chased him, stumbling and picking up handfuls of snow as she went.

I felt very awkward all of a sudden, like I wasn't in on the joke. And I didn't know what to do with my hands or my legs or my whole body, really, so I went over to stand by Mr. Neely.

"Are you having fun, Natalie?" he asked.

I wanted to tell him he looked like a snowman in his puffy white coat and black hat, but of course I didn't, because he is my teacher. I nodded instead. "Are you?"

He laughed and looked at me like I'd said something surprising. "I am. I really am." The boys had attacked him earlier, but he never threw any snowballs back—probably because he was an adult who didn't feel the need to do that, and also probably because he didn't want to get sued.

"Thank you, Mr. Neely," I said. This time I didn't say it because I should, or because I had nothing else to say. This time I meant it. I really meant it.

ASSIGNMENT 24: DAD'S MISSION

Dad woke me up early this morning. "Get dressed," he said, grinning like he'd lost his mind. "We're leaving in fifteen minutes."

I tugged the crusty bits of sleep out of my eyes and managed a mumbly "Fine."

"Oh, and by the way," Dad added, "you aren't going to school today."

I woke up real quick at that, sitting straight up in bed. "What do you mean?" Dad and I hadn't really spoken since my whole Dr. Doris tantrum, and I knew he was pretty much handing me a gift-wrapped chance to make things better.

But Dad just said, "Come on, get dressed. We're going somewhere fun."

One glance at my phone explained everything.[38] Turns out, after #MrNeelysSnowDay, we ended up with a real snow day. This was the best kind of snow day, too, where the weather channel predicts a huge snowstorm, but it doesn't end up snowing that much, and you can still do stuff.

Dad was waiting in the car, windows fogged with the running heater, but Mom wasn't in the passenger seat. I shouldn't have been surprised anymore by Mom's absence, but I still was—every single time. I got into the passenger seat, in her place, running my hand across the leather before I sat, as if I were brushing away her ghost.

When Dad started driving and told me about the snow day, I pretended to act surprised. For one panic-second I thought Dad was taking me to another therapist appointment this week. I'd managed to avoid most of Dr. Doris's Therapist Tricks, but she was definitely onto me, and I didn't know how much longer I could avoid talking about Mom.

But then I realized, no, this wasn't the way to Dr. Doris's. And anyway, this was supposed to be an adventure. We were supposed to be having fun.

"Where are we going?" I asked.

---

38 Text from Twig: SNOW DAYYYYY with a bunch of snowflake emojis.

Dad's grin became his Big Surprise smile, and without even meaning to, I came up with a list of all the wonderful places he could be taking me.[39]

"We're going Christmas shopping!" he said.

"Oh." I tried not to be disappointed, and failed.

Dad noticed and *he* looked disappointed, and the whole car ride felt like one big disappointment, even though neither of us wanted it to be.

"Come on, it'll be fun," Dad said. "We haven't done something fun together in a while." If Dad wanted to do something fun, I could have provided a whole list of ideas.[40] I guess our lives had gotten pretty sad if Dad's idea of fun was running errands.

He looked hopeful, though—so sad and so hopeful—and he was trying, so I told him, "That does sound like fun."

I decided to make that true, too, because if you want something to come true badly enough, sometimes it does.

Christmas was less than a week away, so naturally the mall would be a supremely unfun place to be, especially since everyone else seemed to have the same snow day idea. But we decided to make a game of it by pretending we were warriors marching into battle.

---

[39] In order of least exciting to most exciting: the movies, the aquarium, the arboretum, Six Flags, Disneyland.

[40] See footnote 39.

"Take my hand," Dad said after we got out of the car, sticking his hand out with mock seriousness. I took his hand, even though it was really embarrassing and I was secretly afraid of seeing someone from school. But to tell you the truth, I kind of liked it. I couldn't remember the last time I'd held a parent's hand, and even if we were just being goofy about it, it still felt nice.

By the time we got to the center of the mall, the crowd became too thick. A herd of baby strollers parted the mass of bodies and ripped our hands apart. "Go on, Dad, save yourself!" I said, reaching one hand out and clutching my chest with the other.

Dad laughed, and he came over and bear-hugged me, and people stared but I didn't care. I was too happy. Then we had to get down to business, and it took us one whole hour to buy fancy dinner plates for Grandma.

When we left the kitchenware store, Dad asked, "What would you like to get your mother for Christmas?" I think he meant to sound casual about it, but his words came out wrong. I couldn't blame him. Before, shopping for Mom had been hard because she loved everything. Now it was hard because she didn't love anything at all.

"I don't want to get her something." The words just popped out of my mouth.

Dad's forehead got wrinkly and I could tell he was stepping into Therapist Dad mode in *five, four, three*—

"Or," I began, and Dad got that hopeful look in his eyes again. "Or I guess we could get her another plant."

One crisis averted, another incoming, because Dad's wild *want to be happy* smile was back. "That would be great," he said, as if Mom would care. As if she hadn't killed all her other plants.

I nodded, and looked around awkwardly because we were standing outside Kitchen Kapers, in the middle of the mall, having a Moment.

"Okay, let's go to the plant nursery," I said.

I shoved through the crowds, making my way to the nursery. Mom and I had visited it so many times together that the way to the plants was mapped onto my heart. And despite the crowd and the chaos, I didn't even turn around to make sure Dad was still behind me. I was curling into myself, closing up like sleeping grass, and then someone shouted my name and it took me a second to place the voice, and then—*and then*.

"John! Natalie!" the voice repeated, and I turned to see Mikayla's mom, shouldering her way through the masses, eyes trained on me. She wore her usual jeans and black button-down, with her brown curls loose around her shoulders. The sight of her was so familiar that my heart opened up. And then I remembered what she'd done to my family, and it slammed shut again.

Just that one moment, that split second of happiness,

felt like a betrayal of Mom. I curled my hands into fists and dug my fingernails into my palms.

It took me a moment to spot Mikayla, trailing behind her mother. Because of course. Of course this was my luck. Like I couldn't ever get away from her and just forget about everything.

"Dana! Mikayla!" Dad said, his voice slipping a few notches lower into the tone he uses with Not Our Family.

"John, how are you?" Mikayla said in her wannabe-adult way. She didn't acknowledge me. I didn't acknowledge her. It was as if the whole weirdness last week hadn't happened, as if she hadn't come over to talk to us for no apparent reason at all.

The three of them launched into small talk about the crowd and Christmas and the weather and school—and their words felt like tiny droplets of rain, like the drizzle that says, *Watch out. It's going to pour.*

Finally, Mikayla's mom leaned forward and her eyebrows knitted and she said, "How's Alice?" She said it as if she cared, as if all of this weren't her fault. "We miss her." I'd never hated anyone more than I hated her at that second, and I wished the Christmas crowd would eat her up and carry her far, far away from our family.

Dad hesitated, and I knew I couldn't bear to hear him talk about it, not here, not in front of Mikayla and her mom.

"I'll meet you at the nursery," I said in that tiny moment of hesitation, without looking at any of them. And I was gone before Dad could respond.

I quickly made my way to the plants, slipping through the crowd like a ghost, like I didn't exist at all. And perhaps not too many people buy plants for Christmas, because the store was quiet and nearly empty. I read the descriptions of all the plants on display, because that was better than thinking, but it was that fake kind of reading, where your eyes move and your brain swallows the words without processing them.

Until CAMELLIA JAPONICA 'KOREAN FIRE.' I almost didn't pay attention to the description until I read: BLOOMS THROUGH WINTER, EVEN IN THE SNOW. I read further: THIS HARDY FLOWER CAN SURVIVE IN NEARLY ANY CONDITION.

The Korean Fire. The tiny red flower was not spectacular—not nearly as stunning as a blue orchid—but it seemed right. Maybe we didn't have our miracle plant—yet—but at least we'd have a plant that survives through the winter. A plant that keeps going.

When Dad arrived, we bought the plant. He read the plant name, and then opened and closed his mouth like he wasn't sure what to say. And then, finally, "Natalie, maybe we should talk about—"

But I cut him off. "Can we not do this right now?"

Dad's lips pressed into a straight line, but he nodded. Sometimes when he gets quiet like this, I can tell he's pulling a Therapist Trick, waiting for me to talk and fill the silence with truth. But at that moment, he was just quiet because there was nothing left to say.

We did not talk. We did not hold hands. We just went home.

ASSIGNMENT 25: OBSERVATIONS, ROUND TWO

The snowstorm actually hit today, so we got another snow day. But somehow I still had to see Dr. Doris. Because in Dad's mind, nothing can stop him from pursuing Mental Health. Not even a blizzard.

Anyway, I think Mr. Neely has managed to brainwash me with his hashtags and experiments, because I kept thinking about the scientific process during therapy. Dr. Doris was talking, and I was trying to listen—really, I was—but in my head I was turning her into an experiment.

Dr. Doris said, "Today I want us to talk about your mother."

And my brain went: *Observations!*

- Dr. Doris is wearing bright red lipstick.
- It's snowing so hard today that when we drove here, Dad's windshield wipers had to work overtime, and Dr. Doris's office window is just a wall of white.
- What if the roads shut down and Dad and I get trapped here?
- Dr. Doris asks, "What's on your mind, Natalie?"
- My hands pick up a Slinky on the coffee table, and I watch it go back and forth as if my hands don't even belong to me.
- The plants in this office could use some watering.
- Dr. Doris asks her question again, carefully rewording it because—whoops—I forgot to answer.
- I say, "Nothing."
- Outside, the wind is crying.

Dr. Doris was worried that I wasn't focused during our session, but really, I was just trying to answer my own scientific question: How many questions can I get

Dr. Doris to ask?[41] Naturally, as the success of my experiment depended on getting *her* to talk, I couldn't talk much myself. I think Mr. Neely would be proud. Dad, not so much.

"Okay," Dr. Doris said about halfway through our session. She was probably frustrated. She was probably trying to hide it. "We don't need to talk about your mother if you're not comfortable doing that yet. We can talk about anything you want. What's on your mind, Natalie?"

That was Question Number Twenty-Four. I was busy tallying that question on my mental scoreboard, so that was what was on my mind.

But my *secret* thought was about how Dad had talked to Mikayla and her mom about the "situation," and I didn't know what he'd said and I didn't want anybody else to know about Mom. I felt like maybe it made her look bad, and I didn't want her to look bad, especially in front of the Menzers. Maybe I was embarrassed by her. I didn't want to be.

What I wanted was to stop caring about Mikayla, to shut her out completely. But then I would remember when we were little, hanging out in the lab or the arboretum while our mothers worked. We collected ferns

---

[41] Twenty-three by that point. That woman has some scientific questions of her own.

and sticks to run our own "scientific experiments," which always resulted in incredible cures: Cure for Hiccups! Cure for Homework! Cure for Bedtime!

Cure for Sadness.

And of course our cures always worked, because there was never any other option. We were magic. We were unstoppable. We were scientists.

But now Mikayla is a Cool Girl and I'm not, and it's like Mikayla doesn't even remember the way we used to be. Somewhere along the line, she changed. She turned evil. And I guess Mrs. Menzer must be evil, too, because why else would she fire Mom?

The funny part, though, is that Mikayla's mom was the one who gave me my very own Cobalt Blue Orchid in the first place. She and Mom had been studying the orchid in their lab, trying to figure out how it survived the cobalt and aluminum, trying to apply the findings to other plants, maybe even extend the research beyond plants.

This was in fourth grade, right when Mikayla had just stopped being my friend, and I'd been following Mom around, watching her work, all serious with my hair clipped up, taking notes in my composition book.

"It's pretty," I'd said, admiring the orchid behind its protective glass, trying to describe its papery leaves in my notes, trying to capture the way it looked like any other orchid until the light hit it, and then the flower became so blue it hurt to look at it. I stood there, scribbling and describing and wishing I had one of my very own. And, like a mind reader, Mikayla's mom had gone into their cabinets and pulled out a seed, just for me.

I'd expected Mom to protest—she always talked about how delicate the orchid was, how rare and precious—but she didn't. She just smiled at Mikayla's mom, and something passed between them that I couldn't understand, and then Mom and I had this beautiful, magical plant for our greenhouse.

"Here's a miracle plant of your very own, Natalie," Mrs. Menzer had said. "Study it. Watch it grow."

And we had that orchid until we didn't—until Mom let it die.

Dr. Doris asked another question, and I nodded, even though I hadn't quite heard what she'd asked. In my head, I said: *Twenty-five questions.* And I repeated, *twenty-five, twenty-five, twenty-five,* because I didn't want to think about anything else. And I didn't want to forget my scientific data. If you don't repeat the answers, if you don't hold tight and turn them over and over in your head, one day you'll forget, and then they're lost forever.

"Well." Dr. Doris frowned—but her eyes were a blend of sad and hopeful and something else, too. "That's all the time we have left today. Will you think about what I've said?"

I nodded, and I thought, *Twenty-six.*

After our session, on the drive home, Dad turned down the radio to ask, "How did your talk with Dr. Doris go?"

His voice was about ten notches too innocent, so I responded just as innocently. "It went well," I said, and my voice sounded like sparkles and sunshine in the middle of this blizzard.

He didn't fall for it. "Natalie, I know you aren't happy about the sessions. But I would like you to open up a little."

When he said *open up,* I pictured him ripping open my chest and exposing all my organs, like a dead frog on a lab table. Without meaning to, I flinched.

Dad looked over at me with concern, even though the world had gone white with snow, so he really should have been keeping his eyes on the road. "Things have been really hard for you—for all of us," he said, his eyes returning to the road. "But I do think it's important for you to express yourself."

I almost said I wanted *Mom* to open up and express herself, but I've gotten too familiar with Dad's miserable almost-crying-trying-not-to-cry face, and I didn't want to see it again. Instead, I told him, "I'll try. I promise." I'm mostly sure it was a real promise—because even though I still hated the Dr. Doris appointments, part of me knew he was right. Part of me almost *wanted* to "open up."

And even if I couldn't quite *express* all that, Dad looked over at me, and he smiled.

ASSIGNMENT 26: EGGS IN ACTION

Mr. Neely was the only teacher to assign something over winter break, and his "homework" was simply to keep thinking about our scientific process experiments. Normally, this would mean *do absolutely nothing,* but since the egg drop competition is on January 13, Dari, Twig, and I had our work cut out for us. Our Mission Analyst (aka Dari) reworked some of Twig's ideas, and we'd settled on testing two designs today, before Dari goes to India for the rest of the break.

The school is closed for winter break, so we had to work at one of our houses. And because Dari's parents wanted to meet his new friends and see what he was working on for school, we met at his house. Which made sense, I guess, but was kind of weird because Dad doesn't care what I do as long as it's school-related, and Twig's parents don't care what she does, period, so I'd kind of forgotten that "involved" parents were a thing.

It was too cold to bike to Dari's house, so Dad drove Twig and me over there and then decided to be all responsible and meet Mr. and Mrs. Kapoor. Both of them greeted us at the door when we arrived, while Dari hovered behind them in the house. They were one of those super-in-love couples, and Mr. Kapoor kept his hand on Mrs. Kapoor's back while they spoke—as if he didn't even notice he was doing it. And even though I used to get embarrassed when Mom and Dad did stuff like that—I kind of missed it.

I started to feel that fluttery anxiousness, so I stopped thinking and tried to pay attention to the parents' conversation. Only, they were talking about boring things, like school and the weather. So Twig and I slipped past them to say hi to Dari.

"Okay, goodbye, Yeong-jin and Mr. and Mrs. Kapoor," Twig said as we walked around them. "I'm sorry I don't know your first names yet, but I'm sure I'll learn them soon."

Dari's parents looked at her with matching frowns of confusion, but Dad just sighed as we disappeared into the house.

When we got to Dari's living room, Twig stopped. "This. Is. *Awesome*," she said, taking it in.

And it was: nearly every inch of the walls was covered with family photos and bright, colorful paintings of people, landscapes, animals—anything and everything.

Dari cleared his throat. "Yeah, my parents paint," he said, his tone a mixture of pride and discomfort. "My whole family is full of artists. They kept signing me up for art classes but . . . I wasn't very good at it."

He shrugged. I could tell that bothered him, and I realized there was so much about Dari that I didn't know. I hadn't meant to, but I guess I'd been thinking of him kind of as a teacher—like he only existed in the context of school and our egg drop.

I hadn't made a new friend since Twig, so maybe I'd forgotten how it worked?

Dari led us out of his living room and turned to me as we climbed the stairs. "I didn't know your dad was Asian," he said. I guess there was a lot he didn't know about me, either.

"He's half Korean," I said. "My grandpa was Italian, but I never met him."

"You never talk about being Korean," Dari said, and then I felt weird about it, like I'd done something wrong.

Being in Dari's house, you could tell they were proud

of being Indian. That shouldn't have surprised me, but it did. I mean, Dari never seemed ashamed of it. He actually talks a lot in school about being from India. His mom wears a sari, his kitchen smells like foods I've never tasted, and his whole house is decorated with pictures of his family back in India—aunts and uncles and cousins and his two brothers, who are already adults.

I don't know, it kind of made me feel like my family was bad at being Korean. Like *I* was bad at it. Because, to be honest, I usually forgot that part of me existed until my grandmother visited or someone brought it up. I was only a quarter Korean, and most people couldn't tell just by looking at me. Every once in a while someone would ask about my race, but I mostly just ignored it.

That had never felt wrong until now.

The last stop on our tour was Dari's room, where Indian mixed with American, Bollywood posters bordered baseball posters. And I decided I wanted my bedroom to be all of me, just like that. I promised myself that the next time I saw my grandmother, I'd ask her about Korea.

"We can drop the egg designs from my window," Dari explained as Twig and I walked over to the window to peer out at his setup. Directly under us, in his backyard, he'd laid out a giant tarp and positioned a video camera so that we could play the drops back and examine them.

"Wow, Dari," I said. "This is, um, really intense." And

then, because that didn't seem like enough, I added, "In a good way."

He smiled, then led us back downstairs and into the backyard, eager to show us more of the work he'd done. On their picnic table, he'd already laid out all our materials and drawn up detailed, realistic diagrams for Twig's top two designs.

Twig held up the diagrams, laughing. "But, Dari, where are their *faces*? How will we know what the eggs are feeling?"

Dari looked at me as if he needed me to tell him whether she was joking. I'm pretty sure the idea of somehow upsetting Twig was his personal nightmare. "Um, well, your designs did have a lot of personality, but . . ."

"We like your designs, Dari," I said before he could make things awkward. "And I think they're pretty artistic, too. At least, artistic in a science-y way."

Dari grinned and ducked his head as he grabbed a cotton ball. He pulled the cotton apart, and Twig and I joined him, fluffing white clouds for Cotton Ball Heaven. By the time we got to work on S'meggs, cutting up twigs and marshmallows, Mrs. Kapoor had come outside with mugs of hot chocolate.

"Are you sure you don't want to come in? It's so great to meet Dhairyash's friends," she said, hovering over us for a few extra seconds before going back inside.

"Cotton Ball Heaven"

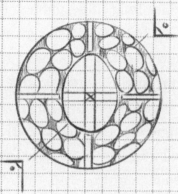

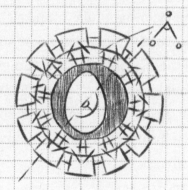

"S'meggs"

I think she felt bad about us working outside in the cold, but we were on a mission.[42] We wouldn't stop, not even to go inside and drink our chocolate. Instead, we warmed our hands against the mugs as we sat around Dari's picnic table. Twig rifled through our egg-building materials and stuffed one of the giant marshmallows in her drink, and Dari and I followed suit. Mrs. Kapoor watched from the kitchen window, and Dari smiled into his mug.

"She's so happy that I finally have friends," he said.

Twig laughed awkwardly, because who admits to not having any friends?

"When I moved here a couple years ago, my parents spoke to all my teachers at Lancaster Elementary and asked them to help me make friends," Dari added, as if it were just some silly story and not at all embarrassing.

"Actually," he continued, even though I kind of just wished he would stop, "that's one of the reasons I did this egg drop. Mr. Neely said I could ask some of the other kids to form a group with me. Of course, I got too nervous to actually ask anybody—until you guys invited me onto your team."

---

42 It probably didn't help that we had to take our gloves off to build the contraption, and Twig kept shouting "MY FINGERS ARE GONNA FALL OFF," even though you didn't see Dari or me complaining. The day was warm for winter—forty-five degrees—and all the snow had melted away.

I figured now was not a good time to point out that he'd actually invited *himself* onto the team.

He smiled hopefully, and I glanced over at Twig, because she was the one who usually started talking in awkward situations, but she'd turned pink and was busying herself by picking apart a marshmallow.

I cleared my throat. "Well, I'm glad you joined us. We wouldn't have been able to do this without you."

I looked around the yard, with Dari's thoughtful, precise setup, and it was *true*. But still—it was a pretty cheesy thing to say.

We all just slurped our hot chocolates and cleared our throats and looked anywhere but at each other for a few minutes.

As soon as I finished my mug, I pushed it aside. "Ready to put the final touches on S'meggs?"

They both looked relieved to change the subject. Twig raised her hand in that silly salute.

We finished up with S'meggs and then got to dropping.

Cotton Ball Heaven went first.

And here's the truth: it broke.

It happened fast: Drop, splat. Dropsplat.

After the failed drop, we stood outside, huddled around the video camera as Dari played it back for us. For the first time, the cold air got to me, and I wrapped my arms around myself.

We watched our egg break in slow motion. The

175

drooooooooooooop, splaaat was way worse when you knew it was coming and watched anyway, waiting without hope.

"The cotton balls weren't thick enough to absorb the impact." Dari paused the camera and pointed to the screen, explaining every single thing we did wrong. "Theoretically, we could add another layer and increase the density here if we need to, but let's test S'meggs and see if that works."

Twig nodded like *yes, yes, tell me more,* but I wasn't listening. I just stared at the frozen egg on the screen, right before the splat. When it was still breakable but not yet broken.

Up until now, the egg competition had been important but far off. It didn't really matter if the eggs broke, because we still had so much time to test them.

Today felt like our last chance, and if both eggs broke today—

"Let's just test S'meggs already," I interrupted my thoughts.

Dari looked up from the camera, surprised at the sudden panic in my voice, but Twig always jumped at the invitation to *go.*

"Got it," she said, running over to grab S'meggs off the picnic table.

We carried our last hope up into Dari's bedroom, and Twig held it out the window, as high as she could.

"I'd like to thank everyone who believed in us and

our egg," she said, addressing an invisible audience as if she'd won some grand award and inexplicably putting on a fake British accent. "I promise we'll remember the little people when we achieve egg drop stardom."

Dari smiled, but I felt a flash of annoyance at Twig—for still acting silly. For not understanding that the time for jokes was over. This moment was dead serious.

I held out my hand to stop her. "Can I drop this one?" I asked, my voice sharper than I wanted it to be.

Twig's eyebrows pinched as she noticed my mood shift for the first time, but she stepped back and handed me the egg. "Sure thing, Captain," she said, her voice just a little uncertain.

I held my breath and then I let S'meggs go—

Drop

Drop

Drop

Drop

And the sound of S'meggs hitting the driveway. But no splat.

We all kind of looked at each other for a minute like, *Do we even dare?*

Dari raced downstairs to inspect our fallen egg—Dari, our calm, collected, studious Dari, running over to our egg like a doctor to his patient.

Twig and I ran after him, breathless while we waited for his analysis, and then he shouted, "It's alive!"

Twig screamed and jumped around, celebrating as if we'd won the Egg Drop Olympics or something. "We're done!" she shouted. "This is the one! This is our winner!"

Dari laughed at Twig's enthusiasm, staring at her with a happy kind of surprise, as if he'd never seen anyone so excited before.

I laughed and cheered, too, because this was exactly what I wanted, and I knew I should've been the happiest of all—but for some reason, the happy feeling turned sticky inside me. Maybe we really would win. Mom and I would go to New Mexico and soak in the miracle of blue flowers and then—and then everything would be okay again. Right? Because if it wasn't—then what?

ASSIGNMENT 27: CHRISTMAS, CRACKED

This morning, I woke up early and ran into my parents' room, shaking them awake just like I do every Christmas.

They were sleepy, and I was too giddy to realize it was anything more than that—too Christmas-happy to realize today was a Bad Day for Mom. Dad said ten minutes. Give them ten minutes, and they would be downstairs. Only, twenty minutes later, Dad came downstairs alone. And I knew: Mom wasn't coming down.

"Look at all those presents," Dad said, gesturing to our tree. "Why don't we open them? We can show Mom later." The way Dad speaks—the way he's *always* spoken—is smooth and rhythmic like one of those old-timey waltzes, but when he said that, I heard anger spike in his voice.

To be honest, that scared me more than anything, because this whole time, Dad has never been angry with Mom. He's been sad and tired and probably a little bit angry with me at times, but never with Mom.

"Come on, Nats." He came over to sit next to me on the couch. "Aren't you excited? It's Christmas!" The anger in his voice was gone by then, but I know what I heard.

I shook my head and turned away. "I'm not excited," I said, and I didn't bother controlling the anger in *my* voice.

Dad sighed and he sounded so old. I'd never thought of my parents as *old*—old in the way of parents, maybe, but not *old*. And then I was mad at Dad, too, because he's a therapist. He helps people for a living, so it's basically his responsibility to help Mom. And if he can't even do that, what is he good for?

I don't know what I was thinking next, but I ran into the kitchen and grabbed a carton of eggs. Before Dad could stop me, I sprinted into our greenhouse, took the eggs out of the carton, one by one, and slammed them into the dead plants. I watched as those eggs exploded, thick globs of yolk soaking into the soil. My little Korean Fire sat in the corner, wrapped in a big, happy Christmas bow, and I threw an egg at that one, too, but I missed.

All of a sudden, I couldn't even find it in me to stand anymore. I dropped the egg I was holding, and it cracked at my feet, and all the energy just seeped from my legs and into the earth. And then I was sitting on the dirt, not even caring about all that egg yolk, and then Dad was next to me, because he didn't care about the yolk, either. The greenhouse floor was warm from the heat lamps, and we sat and stayed sitting.

I kept waiting for Dad to Therapist me, and when he didn't, I handed him the last egg in the carton. He took it and held it up to the light and stared at it as if it were some foreign object. He looked lost. And I thought, *If he throws this egg, I won't know what to do.* Because then look at us: we'd both be sitting in the greenhouse, making a mess, and who would clean it up?

Dad held that egg for a long time, until he finally placed it back in the carton.

And I think, maybe, putting that egg back was even worse than throwing it.

DECEMBER 25

ASSIGNMENT 28: TWIG'S LAUGH

When I heard Dad on the phone downstairs, asking some-one to come over, I thought it was Dr. Doris. Like, maybe she made emergency therapist house calls on Christmas? It couldn't have been my grandmother, anyway, because she was in California this Christmas with her boyfriend, Uncle Gene.

I'd already made the decision not to leave my bed-room, even though I really had to pee, because I didn't want to see Dr. Doris. I didn't want to be Therapisted. But when the knock on my door came, it wasn't Dr. Doris.

Somehow—*Christmas miracle!*—it was Twig.

"Let me in!" She pounded her fist against the wood in her too-loud Twig way.

I jumped up from my bed and opened the door, all my energy-yolk-guts back in me, and when I saw her standing there in a reindeer sweater and jeans with tiny painted Christmas trees, I threw my arms around her and started crying. Kind of embarrassing, thinking back on it, but at that moment, I didn't care about anything except my best friend, standing in my doorway on Christmas.

"Why are you here? You should be with your own family," I said when I'd managed to get myself under control.

Twig took in my tears, opening and closing her mouth. I'd never seen her at a loss for words. But then again, I don't think she'd ever seen me cry.

She inhaled deep and walked over to my bed, hopping onto it as she spoke. "My mom was with me this morning, but she had to work this afternoon." She didn't mention her dad.

Once, we had been friends who told each other everything—even when *everything* was nothing at all. But things have changed. I'm not sure which one of us closed up first.

Twig was uncomfortable—feet tapping against the side of my bed, fingers drumming along my comforter, her whole body full to the brim with nervous energy.

I'd messed up our pattern. I was supposed to say something totally unrelated after that, so the question of her dad wouldn't hang there unspoken, heavy in the air between us. Instead, I sat down next to her on the bed and asked, "Did you talk to your dad today?"

Twig shook her head and bit her lip, and we were quiet for a long time. "He texted to say he'd call later tonight."

"Well, I'm sure he will," I lied. I don't know much about Twig's dad, but I know she's often disappointed.

Twig shrugged. Twig's shrugs mean something matters, but she's pretending it doesn't.

She changed the subject. "Anyway, I came to drop off your Christmas present. I thought your dad hated me, but when I called to see if I could come over, he sounded like he might cry from happiness." She looked at me, waiting for an explanation, and when I didn't respond, she sighed and pulled a small box out of her pocket. "Open it now."

I took the box. It was badly wrapped in newspaper— which meant Twig had done it herself, instead of letting Hélène wrap it in her mom's shimmery foil paper. I knew what it would be—she got the same thing every year—and sure enough, I pulled out a tiny glass figurine. Whenever Twig and her mom went to France, Twig brought back these little figurines. She was obsessed with them for some reason, even though anything so fragile seemed anti-Twig.

This year, she'd given me a tiny green frog.

"In remembrance of Renaldo," she explained.

I smiled, and my chest still hurt, but I felt a little lighter.

"Thanks," I said, setting the frog on my desk and grabbing my present for her. It was an old board game I'd found at a thrift store—of course.

I expected her to open it right away, because normally Twig ripped her presents apart—but she set it aside and turned toward me completely, so she was sitting cross-legged on my bed.

"Natalie. I just—I wanted to say . . ." She took a deep breath. "I know something's going on, and I don't know if it's something I did or if you're sick of me or if you don't want to play board games all the time. We don't have to play board games *at all* if you don't want to anymore. I mean, I can play them by myself or maybe with Hélène, but—"

"Twig," I said, trying to interrupt her, but she was unstoppable when she got going.

"But if I did something to make you mad, I'm really, really sorry. I know I was annoying you at Dari's house, but S'meggs survived, right? So maybe it's okay? I just, I know something's going on, and people don't think I can tell, but I *can* tell, and I just . . ." She stared at me with big eyes, and her mouth opened and closed, searching for more words to fill the silence.

"Twig," I repeated. "It's not you."

I wasn't sure how she could be so right and so wrong at the same time—because of course I wasn't getting sick of her. She was my best friend. I'd just assumed she was *Twig,* oblivious to the rest of the world.

"My mom didn't come out of her room today," I said, blurting out the truth before I could talk myself out of it.

Twig's eyebrows scrunched up, and her eyes filled with sympathy, and she said, *"Oh."*

"It's Christmas, and she didn't come out," I said again, not sure if I was repeating it for her or for myself.

"Natalie," Twig breathed, and I realized then how unfair I'd been. Because the thing was, Twig got what I was trying to say.

And I knew if I kept looking at Twig's face I would cry, so I lay on my bed and rested my head in her lap. She didn't say anything, but she started playing spider-crawling-up-your-back on me, scratching and pounding against my spine, and when she got to cracking an invisible egg on my head, we both kind of laughed and then got serious again.

"And I broke all the eggs in our house," I said.

"Hmm," Twig murmured. "We could have used those eggs."

I surprised myself with a laugh, and when Twig didn't say anything else, I took her silence as an invitation to continue. I forced myself to speak before the words got all gunked up in my throat.

"My mom's depressed," I explained to Twig. The word

depressed felt funny coming out of my mouth. I'd never said it before, and saying it made the whole problem sound too simple.

I felt Twig stiffen for a few moments, trying to figure out what to say, and I worried I'd said too much truth—that I'd scared her away. But then she softened and said, "That's why you've been sad."

I hadn't realized until then just how sad I was, and hearing her say it cracked something open inside me and I started to cry.

"I'm sorry," I said, even though I wasn't sure why I was apologizing. Twig didn't respond, just kept cracking invisible eggs over my head and running streams of fingertip yolk through my hair.

I felt weird about Twig comforting me, because she's *Twig,* so I sat up and pushed her over so she flopped back on the bed. "Hey!" she protested, but she didn't get up. I curled up next to her so we were both lying down, and that felt better. We felt like Natalie and Twig again.

"I thought if we won," I said, "I would use the prize money to fly my mom to New Mexico. If we could get there, and she could see these flowers . . ." I didn't finish, partly because I thought I might cry again, and partly because I felt too embarrassed to finish.

"What flowers?" Twig asked.

So I told her about the Cobalt Blue Orchid, about the

science and its magic. I told her about Mikayla's mom and the lab and how Mom and I grew an orchid all our own, but Mom let it die. I told her the secret hope of my heart—my dream of taking Mom to the miracle flowers and saving her.

"We'll do it," Twig said, and then announced, louder: "We are going to win this thing."

The sigh that came out of me was so loud and long that it didn't sound like me at all.

Twig sat up on the bed, filled with new energy and purpose. "Don't you Natalie-sigh at me. We're winning that contest. We're winning the contest and you're going to New Mexico, and you're gonna get yourself one of those blue flowers—no, you're gonna get *twenty* blue flowers. You could fill your greenhouse with them."

"Twig." I sat up really carefully. Approaching Twig when she got stuck on an idea was like approaching a wild bear. You have to move slowly and speak in a soft, soothing voice.[43] "Calm down. We might win, but we might not." This was something Dad talked about: Managing Your Expectations. "And even if we did, my mom probably wouldn't want to go. She doesn't seem to want to do anything right now."

---

43 At least, that's how I think you'd approach a wild bear, but I've never been camping or anything. Twig and I joined Girl Scouts once for a month in fifth grade, but that didn't last very long. I got bored and Twig kept failing to earn her badges.

I wish I hadn't said that. Saying it felt like a betrayal somehow, like saying it made it true.

"Of course she will." Twig was shifting her weight, left and right, fidgeting with the excitement of a plan. "Once she sees that you did this whole competition just for her, of course she will. Sometimes you need to make one big move to win the game. Sometimes you need to show people how much you love them and then they'll love you back. We can win this, Natalie!"

Twig was getting really excited now. "And, and—even if she *doesn't* want to go, *we* can still go. We can fly all the way to New Mexico and get that orchard!"

"Orchid," I corrected.

"Orchid!"

"Twig," I said slowly, a warning in my voice. "Obviously we can't do that."

"You're right. We can't." Twig winked.

"Twig, no."

"I know." Twig winked again.

I laughed. "Twig, I'm serious!" But I didn't sound very serious at all, not with all the laughing and such.

"Operation Egg is *actually* a secret mission!" Twig shouted, jumping off the bed. With her bugging eyes and messy hair, she was wild in her excitement. "Operation Egg is secretly *Operation Orchard*!"

"No, Twig!" I was laughing so hard my stomach hurt, like when you don't eat a certain food for so long that when you eat it again your stomach starts cramping. That's what laughing had become for me.

"You look so funny when you're laughing like that," Twig said, and then she was laughing, too. "You look like a little snail." She curled up on her side to imitate me, looking nothing at all like a snail.

Twig reached her pinkie out. "I promise you we're gonna win."

I hooked my pinkie with hers and said okay because this moment was too good, and I didn't want to ruin it by being all weird and refusing to pinkie-promise her.

But then I went ahead and did something even *weirder* because this thought popped into my head and I couldn't get rid of it. "Twig," I said, "I think Dari has a crush on you."

Twig got all pink, and she rolled onto her stomach and buried her face into a pillow. "You think he does?" she asked, her voice muffled.

I had never seen Twig like this, but it felt good to talk about something fun. "It's pretty obvious," I said.

She peeked her head up from the pillow to look at me. "I got him a Christmas present, too, but I don't know if I should give it to him."

I tried not to look surprised, because I hadn't even considered getting Dari a present.

"It's a flamingo," Twig added.

And I guess I'd forgotten to turn my filter back on after all that honesty, because without really thinking, I said, "Because he has skinny legs?"

For a second, Twig stared at me in openmouthed horror, and then she rolled over onto her back and started belly-laughing.

And I started laughing again, too, because laughs like that are contagious.

Eventually, Twig had to leave, because her dad actually called, and she went home to talk to him properly. The way she looked at her phone, it was like she got the best Christmas present, and I knew she wanted to get home as fast as she could.

I handed her my present and she hugged me hard. "Remember our pinkie promise," she said into my ear.

When she left, Dad came into my room, all hesitant and hopeful, and I ran over and hugged him. "Thank you, Dad," I said into his chest.

We hugged for a while and he squeezed me so hard I could barely breathe. I didn't mind. I held on tight.

JANUARY 1

ASSIGNMENT 29: *DDUK* LUCK

I woke up early on New Year's Eve—not Christmas-early, but still.

Dad was standing over the stove, scrambling a pan of eggs. Next to him, he had an open carton of eggs, all new and freshly bought. Intact. Uncracked.

"Happy New Year's Eve," he said.

I sat at our table, and he slid the eggs onto two plates, placing them in front of us and sitting beside me.

"Are these eggs some kind of message?" I asked. It was the first time he'd made eggs since Christmas. "Is this a Therapist Trick?" Like, *Look, Natalie! Look what good can come from cracked eggs!*

But Dad said, "It's just breakfast," and I decided to

192

believe that. I took a bite of my Just Breakfast and pretended eggs were just eggs.

"I noticed the Christmas flower you got for your mother is still sitting in the greenhouse." Dad was talking in his fake-happy voice. "You should give it to her today—as a New Year's present!"

Suddenly I felt sick, and the eggs turned funny in my stomach. Dad must have noticed, because he started to get that concerned look in his eyes.

"Maybe later," I said, and when he opened his mouth to say something else, I interrupted fast, with the first thing that came into my head. "I want to make Grandma's *dduk* this year."

And that stopped him right in his tracks. He set his fork down and cleared his throat, but he didn't respond right away.

The thing was, every year, Mom made Grandma's *dduk*. It was our tradition to eat the chewy treat on New Year's—good luck and long life and stuff—but Dad had never made it.

About five years ago, Mom discovered the Japanese tradition of making mochi on New Year's. She'd skipped over to Dad, pointing to a page in the *Foreign Foods!* cookbook she was reading. "We've been missing out on all this luck!" she'd said. "Everybody loves good luck. We should make this with your mom!"

"My mother is Korean." Dad laughed, amused by

Mom's enthusiasm. "Wrong kind of Asian." Dad was eager to play his role. He was the steady one. The one who talked Mom down from her chaos.

But when Mom called Grandma and suggested it, Grandma was all on board. "Good luck is good luck," she said. "But we make *Korean* mochi. *Dduk.*"

Grandma sent Mom a recipe, and Mom Americanized and adapted it, but she called Grandma every year as she made it, chatting about ingredients and measurements and life.

If our family ever needed luck, it was now. S'meggs needed all the help it could get in the egg drop competition. *I* needed all the help I could get.

And if Mom didn't seem interested in making any luck this year, then I would.

Dad pushed his plate of eggs away and forced a smile. "I guess I could ask Grandma for the recipe. You really want to make it?"

If I said yes, Dad would agree, but I could tell he was uncomfortable. I told him yes anyway, I really wanted to make it, so we drove all the way to the Asian supermarket to get adzuki beans and sesame oil. Almost before we even started, mochiko flour got everywhere, dusting the kitchen. Dad got this idea to FaceTime Grandma, and she was all, "HOW CAN I MAKE THE CAMERA SEE ME?" because, you know, grandparents and technology.

I let them fiddle with their phones as I stirred the *dduk* mixture, allowing my muscles to whip the flour and sugar water into a sweet, chewy mass of luck. And when Grandma finally got her phone working, Dad aimed the camera at me so that she could watch.

"Are you counting?" she asked, her voice scratchy with static. "You need to stir one hundred times. One hundred is best."

So I stirred one hundred times, even after Dad offered to take over, even after my arms burned with all that luck.

"*Ipuda,* my beautiful girl," my grandmother said, and that was when I remembered the promise I'd made to myself at Dari's house.

"Grandma," I said, stepping away from the mixing bowl and massaging the ache out of my arm. Dad was holding the phone, so talking to her was almost like talking to him at the same time, but not quite. "Have you heard of the flower Korean Fire?"

She didn't answer for a few seconds, and I thought maybe she didn't hear me, but it was just the phone lag. "Flower? Fire in Korea?"

"No, it's the name of a flower," I said. I glanced up at Dad, whose face was etched with discomfort, but I decided to ask anyway, because this was part of me, too. And I wanted to be the whole me. "It blooms in the snow," I told her. "Even when nothing else can grow."

Grandma nodded. "That is Korean people. We keep going even in the worst time, like when I take your dad to America and we grow, just the two of us. Always growing."

For a moment, I felt like a scientist, gathering little bits of research about myself and trying to analyze it. I looked at my pixely cell phone grandma and said, "Thanks, Halmoni."

Then I glanced over at Dad, afraid to see weirdness on his face—but when we locked eyes, he didn't look uncomfortable. Instead, he looked confused, as if he were hearing the word *halmoni* for the first time.

Parents are strange.

I said goodbye to my grandmother and went back to the *dduk*. Dad and I made little *dduk* balls together. By the time we were done, we had a whole tray of lumpy, squishy, fingerprinty treats, which weren't nearly as good as Mom's, but were still lucky.

We ended up with more of the chewy exterior than the adzuki bean filling, so I took the extra *dduk* and made it long and stringy. I pressed it against Dad's upper lip, giving him a ridiculous bumpy pink mustache. I laughed, and Dad looked at me half amused and half worried, like, *Is there something wrong with my daughter?*

The best part was, Mom came downstairs in the middle of all this, and she smiled at Dad's *dduk* mustache, which made Dad smile for real, which made the *dduk* fall off his face.

"You guys made good luck," Mom said, coming over to us. She leaned against the kitchen counter and crossed her arms over her chest.

"It was Natalie's idea," Dad said, all happy and proud, even though I hadn't done anything at all except suggest doing the same thing we do every year.

"They aren't very good, though," I said. I felt a little self-conscious about them, like maybe she would be disappointed in Dad and me if the *dduk* didn't turn out right.

Mom lifted a piece off the tray and took a bite.

I pressed my fingernails into my palms. Nervous, waiting, worried it wouldn't taste good—that it wouldn't be so lucky after all.

But she smiled that faraway smile and said, "Very impressive."

I tried to picture Mom's old smile, the huge *can't help it* smile, where her top lip curled up a little to show her gums—and I couldn't quite see it anymore.

But at least Mom was smiling some kind of smile, which was good enough. More than good enough, maybe. The smart part of my brain told me not to push my *dduk* luck, but I couldn't help myself, so I launched into the whole story about the baking, from the dough rolling to the FaceTiming. Mom listened and laughed in all the right places (even if it was faraway listening, far-off laughter), and the three of us ate all the *dduk* that day, because we needed all the luck we could get.

And, you know, I think we got it. Because Mom was there and we were happy. All that luck sat in my stomach, tight and full and good, and with all that goodness inside me, I knew I would win this competition. I could do this, because I had Twig and I had Dari and I had *dduk* and I had luck.

ASSIGNMENT 30: OPEN UP

I had another appointment with Dr. Doris today, and even though school doesn't start back up until Monday, this felt like the official end of vacation. No more fun— time for therapy!

Only, therapy was actually really good today, even if that feels weird to admit.

I started off by telling Dr. Doris about the whole *dduk* extravaganza, and I went into detail and really "opened up" and "expressed myself" like Dad told me to. That was easy, I think, because telling the story made me happy. I would have told it again and again if Dr. Doris had let me.

But Dr. Doris wanted to talk about Christmas, too. At first I hesitated, because I was in happy-fun-family mode, but she kept saying, "It's okay to talk to me, Natalie. This is a safe zone."

Until today, my appointments with Dr. Doris had been filled with *Quiet, Natalie. Keep it in, Natalie.* I would hold my breath and count the petals on her wilting flowers and I would watch snow fall outside, but I would not speak.

I would not speak—not about anything real—but the silence pressed around me, and everything that had happened on Christmas pounded in my head, and even though I knew this was a Therapist Trick, I couldn't hold it in anymore.

I told Dr. Doris about how Mom didn't come downstairs, about the eggs and everything. "My present wasn't very good, so I didn't give it to her," I said when I finished.

"What do you mean?" she asked.

I bit my lip, realizing I'd maybe said something wrong. "I shouldn't have gotten a plant. Mom's the plant expert," I explained, "not me." I don't know why I said that.

Dr. Doris waited for me to continue, but I didn't. "What your mother is going through, Natalie, it isn't your fault," she said, and she didn't sound like a therapist. She sounded like a nice lady who was saying something true.

"Why can't everything just be okay again?" The question left my lips without permission. I could've spent a long time scientifically investigating that one.

"You will be okay, Natalie." She said it in that nice-lady, true way again, and for one horrible second, I wished that she were my mother. And then I felt guilty. Maybe that's why Mom stopped loving me, stopped trying for me, because I didn't love her enough. Because *I* wasn't enough.

Before our session was over, Doris asked me to tell my favorite story about Mom, and I realized I couldn't pick just one—because I have a good mother, and I love her, and I've never truly wished for anyone else.

Eventually, I talked about the day in fourth grade when Mom picked me up from school in the middle of the day. Twig was in Paris that week, and Mikayla had been ditching me during lunch, so I was eating alone. And at the end of the week, after I'd cried and told Mom how alone I felt, Mom called the office and told them we had a family emergency.

I didn't realize, at first, what she was doing. During lunch period, I got called to the principal's office, where I sat for twenty minutes and worried about the unknown emergency.

By the time Mom got there, I was all freaked out until she ushered me into the car. "We're going to the arboretum," she explained.

I thought she'd lost her mind. "What's the emergency?" I asked, like maybe she'd forgotten and needed to be reminded that our family was in danger.

But she laughed and waved her hand. "There is no emergency. I just thought you deserved a day off, and I missed my favorite daughter." In my memory, she is made of sunlight and fresh air.

We drove to the arboretum, and she told me about every single plant we saw, and it wasn't even boring because she had a way of making things fascinating. "This is a willow," she said, running her hand along a thick, tall tree trunk, "the goddess tree. The bark has been used to heal for many, many years. It's sometimes called 'nature's aspirin.'"

When we passed the herbs, she knelt at the sage, fingering the silvery-green leaves. "The wisest herb," she said with a wink. "Eating it increases brain function."

As we wandered through the leaves and trees and flowers, I picked my favorites[44] and she said "Good choice" for everything I listed. When we reached the end of the path and sat on a giant log in the middle of the woods, she pulled me against her and told me about the Cobalt Blue Orchid.

She told it to me like a legend or a myth. "This is a

---

44 Lavender and lady ferns and sweet violet.

flower that achieved the impossible," she told me. "This flower survived in the face of chemicals and toxins, and it turned all that death into something beautiful. That miracle field, Natalie, that's the happiest place in the world."

And when Mom talked about the orchids, she came alive, more alive than I'd ever seen her before. This was the first time she'd told me about her research, and even though I'd read about it in her book, hearing her talk about it, I truly understood the meaning of those words— the magic of her passion.

"Imagine what we could do with this orchid," she said. "We have this flower that can grow in the face of toxic chemicals. If we could find some way to harness that healing ability and apply it to human cells—that would more than be a miracle."

As she spoke, the flower became more and more magical, until I didn't care about lavender or lady ferns. The Cobalt Blue Orchid became my favorite flower in the world. And that day was my favorite day.

Two weeks later, when Mikayla's mom gave me my very own seed, Mom and I planted it together, very carefully, in perfect conditions, so it would bloom just for us. So it would soak up all the toxins in our lives and save us.

When I finished telling the story, Doris smiled and said, "What a beautiful memory," and I smiled and nodded back as if that's all it was. I tried not to show how excited the memory had made me, because I didn't want to raise any Red Flags,[45] but inside I was bubbling with hope.

I'd been Managing My Expectations. But now I was full of luck and Mom was laughing again and we were almost a Happy Perfect Family.

I could win this competition. I *would* win. And finally, after months and months of darkness, Mom and I would have another flower. We would regrow that magic.

---

[45] Red Flags, *n.*: possibly therapists' favorite term in the world. They see them everywhere. Trust me, I know.

ASSIGNMENT 31: OBJECTS IN MOTION

MATERIALS:

- 3 washers
- 3 strings
- Scissors
- Tape

PROCEDURE:

1. Cut each string to a different length: short, medium, long.
2. Tie a washer to one end of string and tape other end to table.
3. Bring washer up to desk height and drop.
4. Record number of swings.

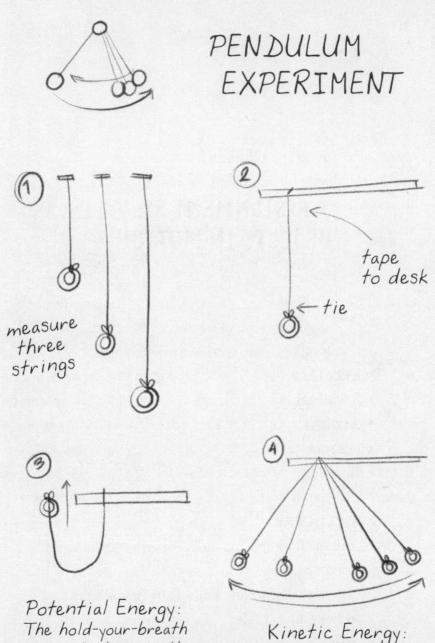

PENDULUM EXPERIMENT

1 measure three strings

2 tape to desk ← tie

3 Potential Energy: The hold-your-breath moment where anything seems possible.

4 Kinetic Energy: The energy of motion. A force that seems unstoppable.

RESULTS:
- Dari's string, long: 16 swings
- Twig's string, medium: 23 swings
- Natalie's string, short:

Today was the first day back in school after break, and Mr. Neely seemed determined to pump up our energy.[46] If we thought Mr. Neely loved dead frogs and magnets, we experienced a whole new level of Neely love today. We walked into class to see *#NewtonInMotion* written in giant letters on the whiteboard.[47] A weird YouTube song called "Objects in Motion" blasted on the speaker. Even suck-uppy Mikayla was shocked into silence.

Across the room, Twig started playing air guitar and rocking out to Mr. Neely's nerdy music, and Dari joined in and played the air piano, because I guess the piano was the coolest instrument Dari could think of. Everyone stared—especially at Dari, because he was usually so serious in class—and I felt half embarrassed and half proud, because I had the weirdest friends in the seventh grade.

Mr. Neely clapped along, beaming at their jam sesh, and when the music ended, he introduced our experiment

---

[46] Pump up our *kinetic* energy, that is.

[47] Do you think Isaac Newton would be proud or alarmed that his famous laws have been turned into a hashtag?

of the day: washer pendulums.[48] Dari, Twig, and I set up on our table in the back, and Dari started telling us about his trip to India while we worked. Dari, of course, could finish his pendulum while he told his stories, but Twig and I kind of gave up working and listened to him talk about his brothers, who tried to teach him to skate-board.[49]

As Dari spoke, I started thinking about my own family, which meant thinking about Mom. And then I thought about the egg drop in a few days, and how important it was, and I started feeling a little head-spinny.

"Oh, by the way, guys," Dari said, looking at me as if he'd read my mind—or maybe he'd just noticed I was distracted. "I was working on S'meggs a little more and I added just a few tweaks. We didn't test it from the height it'll actually be dropped from, so I adjusted the angles a bit."

"That's great, Dari," Twig said, and then cleared her throat and glanced over at me. She'd been mostly nor-mal since our conversation on Christmas, but she always looked a little nervous when the competition came up.

"Tweaks?" I asked. The spinning feeling got worse.

---

48 Washers, *n.:* possibly science teachers' favorite thing in the world.
49 A story about skateboarding sounds cool and everything—until you remember it's Dari. Because of course he managed to make it nerdy by relating it back to science and talking about momentum and stuff.

"They aren't a big deal," Dari reassured me. "You won't even notice. But they should help the egg survive impact."

"We'll win this thing," Twig said, a little too intensely. "Dari knows what he's doing."

Dari looked between the two of us, trying to figure out what we weren't saying, but I was saved by Mr. Neely, clapping his hands and announcing, "Five more minutes, class!"

Dari jumped a little and looked down at our unfinished pendulums in horror. I don't think he was used to getting distracted during class. He worked fast to finish all three of the pendulums.

"Well done, us," Twig said. She picked up her washer and dropped it, and we all watched it swing back and forth, back and forth, as if we were getting hypnotized. "Twenty-three swings," Twig announced when the pendulum stopped, and we all paused to record the number. Then came Dari's turn, with a total of sixteen swings.

And here, just to prove I learned something today, is the scientific concept of the pendulum: once an object is in motion, it either transfers its energy to another object or keeps moving for all of eternity. Based on the laws of physics, if our pendulum was placed in a vacuum, it would never stop swinging, back and forth, back and forth.

The problem with Earth is there's gravity, and atmosphere, and all that other sticky, tricky Earth stuff that slows the pendulum down until it stops. So, basically, nothing works as well in real life as in theory.

Class ended before we had time to test my pendulum. Dari gasped in horror and said, "I'll have to run this experiment at home," while Twig said, "We'll have to make something up."

"Sorry, guys," I said, even though I wasn't really sorry. And secretly, as Twig and Dari were cleaning up and getting back to their desks, I started my pendulum, swinging fast on its short string. It looked wild, frenzied, like it wasn't sure which way to go, forward and back, forward and back, and before it could slow down, I clamped my hand over the washer. I didn't care if I couldn't record the swings. I didn't want to see it stop.

STEP 7: RESULTS

All your hard work has paid off! Now reap your rewardz! Record the results of your experiments. Remember: there are no losers in #science #life.

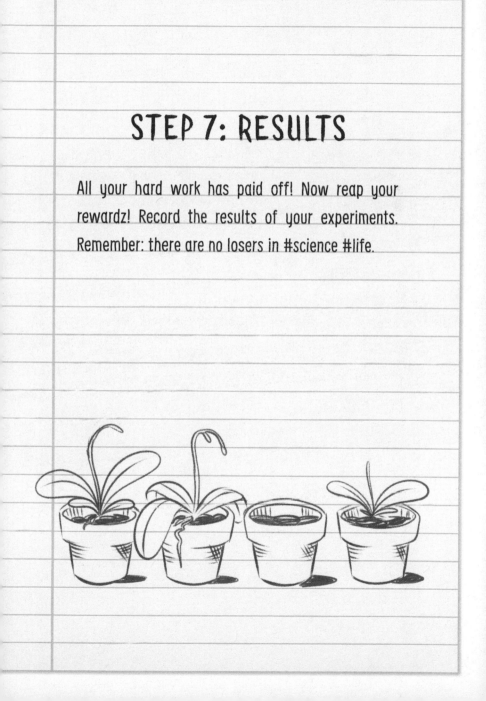

ASSIGNMENT 32:
FLY, LITTLE S'MEGGS!

On the morning of the egg drop competition, while Dad prepared for his afternoon work sessions, I stood outside his and Mom's bedroom.

I almost went in. But I did not. And Mom did not come out.

More than ever, I knew how important this competition was, and I knew we had to win. I wanted to go inside, tell her what a big day this was—I wanted to make her understand and make her feel. But I couldn't get my hand to turn the knob.

Dad came out of his office and found me standing in front of their bedroom door. "Natalie," he said, ready to launch into some Therapist Talk.

But I pointed at the clock and interrupted with, "We're gonna be late," and went to wait for him in the car.

When we finally got going, we swung by to pick up Twig, who burst into the backseat of the car and greeted us: "We are going to *kick* butt."

Dad glanced at her in the rearview mirror, probably deciding whether or not to scold her for language, but then she leaned forward, toward the passenger seat, so her breath tickled my ear.

"I promise you," she said in an almost-whisper, "we're gonna win this. I can feel it."

At her words, my stomach twisted in excitement—because as much as I was still trying to Manage My Expectations, I couldn't help it. We *were* going to win. I could feel it, too, in the air around us.

We finally got to the competition, and I don't know if I was expecting some grand ballroom or whatever, but the egg drop was hosted at an old three-story building. The second and third floors had a collection of random businesses, but the entire bottom floor used to be a library. Now it's apparently used to host community science events.[50]

Dad parked, and Twig and I looked up at the roof, where S'meggs would be put to the test. "I'm so proud

---

50 Do you think there's any significance to this? Like, move over, books, SCIENCE IS THE FUTURE.

of you two," Dad said—and I felt almost guilty, for the first time, because Dad had no idea why I was really doing this.

I tried not to think about that, and the three of us went inside.

"This place stinks," Twig said. "It smells like old people and wet carpet, but stronger—like fifty old people and piles of wet carpet."

"Ew," I said.

"Yeah." Twig grinned, pleased with her description.

Dad put a hand on each of our shoulders and said, "It's not that bad," but he was frowning as he said it.

"Okay, Yeong-jin," Twig said, and Dad's frown deepened.

The entire floor was still set up like a library, with rows and rows of shelves, but they were empty, and when we spoke, our words echoed along the concrete floors, vibrating against the ghosts of old books.

The room was already packed with kids and their parents—and I realized I'd never thought about the other teams. I'd figured once we had a good egg, that'd be it, and the money would be ours. Nervousness bubbled up in my stomach, and I buried my hands in my coat pockets and stuffed that worry back down.

A lone microphone stand was propped up in a corner of the room, but we weren't given any instructions and nobody seemed to be in charge. The abandoned library felt too loud and too hot.

Dari was supposed to be there already, and the minutes kept ticking by, and fluttery panic bloomed in my chest. I shouldn't have let him keep S'meggs, but he'd wanted to hang on to it, and I hadn't said no, and now if he didn't show up, we wouldn't be able to participate and I couldn't win the money, and—

The doors opened and Dari walked in with both of his parents behind him.

"It smells weird in here," Dari said when he reached us.

So of course Twig gave him the same description she'd given me, word for word. They launched into a discussion about why the room smelled like old people and wet carpet when there was, in fact, no carpet in the room, but I cut them off.

"Did you bring S'meggs?"

Obviously Dari did, because Dari's smart, and forgetting the egg at an egg drop contest would be a not-so-smart move, but the question got them back on track. "I made a few more tweaks last night," Dari said. "I reasoned that tightening the inner angles would allow the egg to handle a bigger impact."

I wished Dari had stopped making these "tweaks." But I told myself to breathe. I mean, Twig was right: he was the smartest kid in our class. He probably knew what he was doing.

Within fifteen minutes, so many people had shown up that the room got hotter and more humid and even smellier. Mr. Neely arrived and waved his arms when he saw us, weaving in and out of the other teams as he made his way over.

"What an exciting day!" he said to us after he'd shaken hands and introduced himself to Dad and the Kapoors.

"We're going to win," Twig informed him.

"Of course you are—you're my scientific explorers!" he said. I couldn't tell if he was serious or not.

"I'm the head sheriff, and Dari is the mission analyst," Twig continued matter-of-factly, and I wished she would stop. Those titles were just a joke, after all.

Mr. Neely grinned. "Well, of course. Every team needs a head sheriff and a mission analyst."

"Natalie is the team captain," Twig said.

Mr. Neely beamed at me, and Dad reached over and squeezed my shoulder, and I just wanted to disappear.

"I'm glad to see you're taking charge, Natalie," Mr. Neely said. And then, to our parents: "These three are my top students."

That definitely wasn't true, but it was nice of him to say.

He talked with our parents for a bit, about how he left his pharmaceutical research job to teach. When he went to talk to the other science teachers, I watched him interact with them. He was still his awkward self, but he wasn't *ours* anymore. It was weird, and all of a sudden I felt angry. Like, he was supposed to be our teacher and that was it, and now he was this *person,* with friends and a past in pharma-something-whatever.

He was living a double life, and maybe the Mr. Neely we knew wasn't completely real.

Then I realized I was being ridiculous, so I took a few breaths and tried to calm down.

Eventually, a tall woman with glasses stepped up to the microphone. Finally, somebody was in charge and giving us direction. "Welcome, young scientific minds of Lancaster! My name is Charlaine." Charlaine looked like Doris, only ten years older and a twinge more Southern, and for some reason, the comparison made me itchy with discomfort.

"I know how hard y'all have worked on your egg drops," she continued, "and I want to tell you, first and foremost, you are all winners!"

Dari nodded along, but Twig looked at me and rolled her eyes because this Charlaine woman was being a Mr. Neely. She pointed to her chest and then mine and mouthed, *Winners.*

Charlaine went on to introduce the other five judges, but I was too busy eyeing the competition to pay attention. Most were uninspired inverted egg cartons. Ours was definitely one of the best designs.

I felt better seeing everybody else's eggs, and when

Charlaine and the other judges started setting up, Twig, Dari, and I abandoned our parents and walked around the room to get a closer look.

"You did a really nice job with the tweaks, Dari," Twig said, admiring the contraption in Dari's hands.

Dari blushed. "Thanks, but you're the one who had the great idea for S'meggs."

I sighed—I couldn't help it—and then they both turned red, and all three of us kind of wanted to disappear for a few seconds.

As we made a lap around the library, a pair of redheaded twin boys stopped us. "What a *creative* design," the first one said. They were dressed in matching sweaters stitched with the Valley Hope crest, and it took me a moment to realize they were talking to us.

"I would never have considered marshmallows," the second twin continued. "How *cute*." They spoke in that fancy Valley Hope way, enunciating their consonants and rounding their vowels, and it was hard to tell whether they were sincere or sarcastic.

"Thank you," Dari said, polite by reflex. "Clever design yourself."

I glanced down at the contraption in the first boy's hands, and my heart seized up and settled in my throat. They had cushioned the egg in cotton balls and placed it into a ziplock bag full of Lucky Charms cereal.

Twig gave Dari a look of disappointment and stepped

forward. "Cereal is a stupid idea," she said. "S'meggs is gonna beat your egg."

The first twin said, "S'meggs?" and the second stiffened and said, "May the best egg win," before they took their cereal and walked away.

Twig turned to Dari and said, "Did you see that? Did you see that?" As if maybe he could have missed the entire exchange.

Dari mumbled a response, but I tugged on her hand. "Twig, let it go," I said.

She frowned, but for once she actually listened.

To be honest, I'd forgotten about Mom's cereal idea until that moment. Or if I hadn't forgotten, I'd at least buried it deep with all the things I wouldn't say, and I stood there for a few minutes, watching Twig ramble on without really hearing her. I don't know what our egg dropper would have looked like if Mom had helped us, if she had been happy and real and full of experiments. But I guess I wouldn't have been at this competition at all if that were the case.

I tried to put the cereal out of my mind. S'meggs would win, and that was all that would matter in the end.

The judges passed around a bowl for drawing out numbers, and as the team captain, I took a slip. Number 16. The 1 and the 6 still smelled like Sharpie, and I folded it into a tiny square in my palm. Out of the twenty teams, we'd be one of the last to go.

The drop would happen off the roof into a designated spot in the parking lot, so after drawing our numbers, we all shuffled into our winter coats, rewrapping and bundling and buttoning, until we were standing outside in the parking lot, breathing hot air into our mittened hands. The judges took our eggs up to the top of the building, except for a young curly-haired judge with a name tag that read SHAWN. He stayed below to announce the status of dropped eggs: Cracked or Not Cracked. A few contestants tried to make conversation with him, but I tuned them out, bouncing on the balls of my feet, battling the cold and my nerves.

"We'll be fine," Twig said, calm as could be.

"This is much higher than our test at my house." Dari clenched and unclenched his hands, buzzing with nervous energy.

"Our egg is strong," Twig said as Charlaine announced the first egg and dropped it off the edge of the roof.

It broke, and I let out a sigh of relief.

With so many contestants, the drops took a while, interspersed only occasionally with the cheers from a surviving team. Later, the judges would score the surviving eggs based on *durability* and *bounce factor* and *aerodynamic design*. We'd survive, too—I just knew it.

Somewhere along the way, Twig slipped into Announcer Mode, whispering observations into Dari's and my ears.[51] She spoke in a low voice and said stuff like, "The Blondes are tense with anticipation. Will their Bubble Wrapped egg make it past the Drop of Doom? The crowd holds its breath—hold your breath, guys—and, wait for it, our fearless Charlaine is about to drop the egg and—ohhh, close but no cigar. This is a tough break for our Blondes. Literally." The kids around us turned to glare, and eventually some random parent came up and told us to please be quiet, which was embarrassing for Dari and me, but of course Twig didn't mind at all.

Listening to Twig's commentary, I could get through most of the round without too much anxiety, but by the thirteenth egg, none of us spoke. Instead, the three of us held hands with the number 16 pressed between Twig and me, and it wasn't even weird or embarrassing. This abandoned library parking lot was like an alternate universe where everyone really cared about raw eggs, and holding hands was a totally acceptable thing to do.

When Charlaine got to our number, I looked over at Dad and he gave me a big, goofy thumbs-up. Twig squeezed my hand so hard I was pretty sure all my bones shattered.

In that moment, when everything stood still and the outcome was unknown and all of us were hopeful, I got this huge surge of love for Dad and Twig and Dari. For

---

51 Although Twig isn't really capable of whispering. Being quiet isn't her strong suit.

Mr. Neely and even Dari's parents and all these people who were making my life so much better. I wanted to hug each one of them, but I didn't want to get sappy, either. I missed Mom, of course, but the weird part was that I didn't feel angry or sad or uncomfortable about missing her, like I usually did. Instead, I felt hopeful, partly because winning seemed so inevitable and I had big plans for that money, but also because if my world could be so happy just because of a silly little contest and the fate of an egg, then I knew Mom's world could be happy again, too.

She would be okay because we would win and I would save her.

Charlaine dropped our egg.

My heart burst into Super Panic Mode and in my head I said, *I'm okay, I'm okay, I'm okay.* But this was different from dropping the egg with Twig and Dari. Then, it had been only us, and we had only been experimenting. Now everything was out of our control.

My heartbeat thudded in my ears.

And S'meggs hit the ground.

The twigs went flying, bits of marshmallow exploded, and a cloud of glitter burst in the air.

We didn't need to wait for Shawn's announcement. The *sound* it made was enough. That cracking, crunching noise was the loudest sound I've ever heard in my whole life.

I looked at my friends because I didn't want to look at the puddle of yellow, growing bigger and bigger around our egg. The broken sticks were like broken bones.

Dari was shaking his head, back and forth, back and forth, like he didn't even know he was doing it, but Twig was still.

"The glitter was supposed to be a surprise," she murmured, in a voice far too quiet for Twig. Still, she did not move, and I had this scary thought that maybe she would never move again.[52]

Dad and Dari's parents came up to us, and Dad put a hand on my shoulder. "Do you want to go?"

Twig answered for me. "Yeah, we don't need to see those stupid Valley Hope kids win." She was shaking with fury and disappointment, so I guess she was moving again, but not in the way I wanted her to.

"Wait," I said. "I want to wait."

One summer day, a rare one when she wasn't working, Mom had taken me to the local pool. We'd been talking about sound waves, and to demonstrate the difference in water, she'd concocted an experiment.

"Ready?" she'd asked as we both hung on to the edge of the pool. And I'd said, "Ready," and we'd slipped under the water. She said a sentence, and the water molecules

---

52 Not literally never move, obviously, but never move again in the way of Twig, like maybe she would be Not-Twig from now on, like Mom was Not-Mom. I don't know. I was in Super Panic Mode.

twisted and morphed the sound, and when we both emerged, I had to guess what she'd said—had to find meaning in that garbled underwater language.

That was how my words sounded to me at that moment.

"Okay," Dad said. "We'll wait." His hand hadn't left my shoulder, and he squeezed hard, as if to remind me I was still there.

Around me, Twig and Dari and Mr. and Mrs. Kapoor were speaking, but I couldn't quite hear them. Mrs. Kapoor knelt next to Dari, and her yellow sari, the color of bright, fresh yolk, peeked out from underneath her long down jacket.

Charlaine was somehow still carrying on with the competition. I watched as another egg dropped, another egg broke, and I counted: *Seventeen, eighteen, nineteen.*

Dad kept holding on to my shoulder, and I kept counting, and Dari said into my ear, "It's always good to see the results."

I nodded vaguely, even though I wasn't really seeing. I was waiting.

And then it was the Valley Hope twins' turn. I couldn't see the cereal all the way up on the roof. I could only see the ziplock bag.

My feet and hands were completely numb with cold, but I didn't bother trying to warm them up.

Charlaine dropped the cereal egg.

And this time, there was no crack. Only the crunch of Lucky Charms.

I couldn't breathe. I was back underwater. I thought, *I should have listened to Mom.*

"What?" Dari asked, and I realized I'd spoken that out loud.

Shawn stepped forward to inspect the egg, and my head rang with *Mom would be so disappointed in me*—but then he gave a thumbs-down. Cracked.

The egg was broken.

The egg had a tiny fracture, hardly noticeable, but its life was oozing out, just like all the other broken eggs. So Mom was wrong.

And that was worse.

"Yes!" Twig shouted, and the crowd turned around to glare at her. Twig lowered her voice, but only a little. "I told them cereal was a stupid idea."

The crowd started rustling around us, and Shawn announced that anybody who wanted to stay for the final deliberation could wait inside the library.

I heard myself say, "We can leave now."

All of us kind of adjusted and readjusted our clothes, saying goodbyes, all long and drawn out, because we wanted to leave, but we also weren't ready to go.

Mr. Neely came up and gave us hugs and tried to act happy even though we obviously weren't. "I'm so glad you guys participated," he said, and I wanted to cry at the word. *Participate,* as if that was all we were capable of.

"I have to say, your design was my favorite." He winked. "So creative and inventive. What Charlaine said earlier is true—you three are winners, no matter what. You've worked so hard, and you've learned so much about the scientific process. I'm proud to be your teacher."

Dari blushed and mumbled a thanks, and Twig stared up at Mr. Neely in shock, because I don't think she's used to praise from a teacher. Beneath all the numbness, anger sparked inside me, heating inside my chest, because Mr. Neely had *no idea.* He stood there, talking about the scientific process—as if that mattered. As if his stupid science experiment had anything to do with real life.

"Let's go," I said, and turned to walk away without waiting for a response. Dad was probably horrified by my rudeness—I was sort of horrified, too—but I had to get away.

Twig and Dari ran after me, and Twig grabbed my arm. "This can't be it, though. Operation Egg can't be *over.*"

I shrugged. I knew the sadness would come later, but at that moment, I was upset and a little bit nauseated— anger on an empty stomach.

Dari got quiet, too, and he whispered, "We'll still be friends, right? After this."

Twig looked like she'd cry, and we were all Not Okay.

"Of course we will," she said, first to Dari, staring straight at him, and then she turned to me. Her eyes lit with a fire deeper and bolder than I'd seen in her. "Of course we will."

She hugged me and I hugged her back, holding on tight. I felt kind of bad because I knew Dari felt awkward and out of place, but I couldn't stop hugging her. Twig was my best friend and I needed her.

When we pulled away, her eyes were fierce. "Operation Orchard is still on. We can still fix things," she said.

I sighed and shook my head. "It's over, Twig," I said. I couldn't think about the orchid. I couldn't even look at her. I felt the sadness growing inside me, and if I thought about what this meant, that sadness would take root and never leave.

Dari didn't ask, but he looked at us, questions and half answers dancing in his eyes.

"But—" Twig said.

I cut her off. "It was a stupid idea anyway," I said. I brushed past her and got into the car, slamming the door in her face.

ASSIGNMENT 33: OPERATION ORCHID

The car ride home was awkward, to say the least. I didn't speak. Dad didn't speak. And Twig didn't speak.

Not until, finally, as we drove down that long road to Twig's house, Dad said, "I'm sorry the drop didn't work out like you'd hoped. Would you guys like to talk about it?"

I thought the answer was pretty obviously *no,* but Twig was the one who responded. "Natalie doesn't want to talk right now, Yeong-jin. And that's okay."

I could feel her looking at me, but I kept myself turned away, looking out the window at the bare trees.

I kept silent while we dropped off Twig, silent the whole way home, even though I could feel Dad's tension growing, pressing in on me from all sides. I knew I should say something, because that was the Right Thing to Do, and I should be a Good Daughter, but if I acknowledged what happened, I'd be swept away in that tidal wave of hopelessness.

When we got home, I went right upstairs to my room and wrote about what happened, and lay in my bed and tried to go to sleep—even though it was only seven o'clock. Dad came knocking, but I didn't respond, and he drifted away, trying to "give me space."

And as I lay in bed, my mind swung back and forth—even when I tried to silence it—and it spun and spun, pointing in all different directions.

I told my brain to be quiet and checked my phone.

Twig: CALL ME!!!

I sighed and tossed my phone across my bed. For some reason, I kept thinking about Mr. Neely and *taking charge*—and I'm not sure how, but apparently I managed to fall asleep, because I woke up to the sound of my phone ringing.

I fumbled for my phone in the dark and managed a "Hello?"

It was the middle of the night. I was tucked in, surrounded by all my favorite pillows, and a glass of milk sat on my bedside table. I took a deep breath and shook my head, forcing out the sleepiness and the memories from earlier that day that kept slamming into me.

"Finally! This is my fifth time calling!" Twig's voice blared into my ear, and I turned the volume down on my phone. "I know you probably still don't want to talk right now, and that's okay, but just let me do the talking. Because I couldn't let the plan die. Not like that. And I was thinking and thinking about it—and I think there's a way to get the flower."

I knew from experience not to pin much excitement on Twig's big ideas—but it was so tempting. Maybe Twig had found a way to fix everything. Maybe I hadn't lost everything just yet. "Really?" I asked. My voice sounded breathless.

"I stole my mom's credit card," Twig explained. "We can go to the airport and buy plane tickets, and we'll bring an orchid back for your mom."

And just like that, my hope wilted. I should have known better. This reckless plan was totally Twig. It would never work.

"Twig," I said, trying to keep the disappointment and anger from rising in my voice. I was frustrated with myself, more than anything—for hoping. It wasn't her fault. "That's a terrible idea. We can't just hop over to New Mexico for the night."

"But we have to! We have to go to New Mexico because that's where you got the orchid in your greenhouse. And we have to replace it because you've been so sad—"

"Twig, wait." Suddenly everything clicked into place. All night, my mind had been spinning in circles, and now, finally, it stopped, pointing in one obvious direction.

Because of course we could still get the Cobalt Blue Orchid.

After all, I *hadn't* gotten the greenhouse orchid from New Mexico. I'd gotten it from Mom's lab. And that was only a short bus ride away.

It was such an easy answer, yet it had never crossed my mind. The betrayal of going back to the place that hurt Mom—the place that had thrown her away like she didn't matter—was almost too painful to consider. Just the idea of being back there twisted my stomach. But I would be doing it for Mom, so I pushed away the ache. If I couldn't bring her to the orchids, I would bring an orchid to her.

"Twig, wait," I said again, gripping the phone so tightly that my fingers started going numb. "We don't have to fly to New Mexico. There are seeds in my mom's lab. I can go there—I can go there *tonight.*"

Twig yelped, and I had to turn down my volume even more. "The lab at Lancaster University? *Natalie!* Why didn't you say so? We can do that. We can do that!"

"Twig, no," I said, already climbing out of bed. "You're not coming."

I turned on my lamp and tiptoed through my room,

grabbing a notebook and pen. The clock read 12:56 a.m. I had no time to lose.

"What? Of course I'm coming!"

"Twig, no," I repeated. This whole time, I'd let Twig and Dari take the lead on the egg project. But now I needed to *take charge.* And I couldn't drag my friends into this.

"But—"

I hung up and turned my phone on silent. I knew she'd be upset about this, but I couldn't risk it. Breaking into Mom's lab would be hard, and I didn't want Twig to get in any trouble.

I pulled up the Lancaster transportation schedule on my phone and tap-tapped my way to the bus times, and I came up with a plan. I leaned over my notebook and wrote down a quick procedure, because if Mr. Neely taught me anything, it's to be thorough:

PROCEDURE:
1. Steal Mom's lab keys.
2. Walk ten minutes to the nearest bus stop.
3. Catch the 1:23 a.m. bus, ten stops to Garden Springs.
4. Walk the five blocks to Mom's old lab on campus.
5. Break in and steal an orchid seed.
6. Catch the 2:48 bus home.

I ripped out the notebook paper and stuffed the procedure in my pajama pocket, and felt a giddy thrill rising inside me. There should have been a moment, I think, where I went, *Oh, wait.* But I hadn't just silenced my Bad Idea Alarm. I'd broken it. And here was the solution to Not-Mom, the answer I'd been hoping for since the summer.

For the first time, I was doing something real. The egg drop was full of wanting and wishing and hoping. Now here I was—*doing.*

First step: grab Mom's keys. I tiptoed through the dark, silent house and stood outside Mom and Dad's room, turning the knob all the way before I pushed the door open.

In the darkness of their room, I could barely make out their outlines—Mom curled up against Dad, and Dad holding her gently, even in sleep, as if she were breakable. As if she weren't already broken.

I took a deep breath and crept toward their dresser, where Mom left her purse at night. It was a big bag because Mom used to lug her whole life around with her, wherever she went. She hadn't used the purse in a while. She hadn't gone anywhere in a while. I opened the latch to her purse and dug through the pockets—*Quick, Natalie. Quiet, Natalie*—and then there they were: the cold, solid keys, resting right in my hand.

I wrapped my fist around them so they wouldn't clink, and left my parents' bedroom with three wide, breathless steps. I hurried back down the hallway, the keys biting into my palm the whole time, and I'd almost made it to my bedroom door when I heard someone clear their throat behind me.

ASSIGNMENT 34: TEAM CAPTAIN

I turned, stomach dropping to my feet. I wasn't ready to face my parents, wasn't ready to be stopped. Not when I was so close.

But it wasn't Mom or Dad standing behind me. It was Twig.

I had to clap my hand to my mouth to stop a yelp of surprise from escaping.

"Hi," Twig whispered. Her blond hair poked out from under a black beanie, and she smiled her wild Twig grin.

It took me a moment to orient myself, to understand that she was standing in my room, in the middle of the night. "Twig? How did you get in here?"

She waved her hand through the air, swatting away

my question as if it were ridiculous. "I've been your best friend for years. Of course I know where your parents hide the spare key." Twig was whispering, but we all know by now that whispering is not her strength.

I glanced back at my parents' bedroom, holding my breath, but the house was silent. "You know about the fake rock?"

Twig gave me a look like, *duh.* She was wearing all black—leggings, boots, beanie, and her big puffy coat, which rustled as she moved closer to me. "What's the plan? Are you ready to go?"

"Twig, I—"

She held her hand up as if to physically stop my protests. "I know you told me not to come, but I'm your best friend in the whole world. I'll always be by your side. And besides, this is the best adventure ever. I'm not getting left behind."

My heart was so full in that moment that I wanted to cry, but I just wrapped her in a hug instead. Truth is: I felt better knowing Twig was there. Twig made everything seem possible.

I pulled the procedure out of my pocket and handed it to her.

She scanned it quickly and looked at her watch.[53] "If

---

[53] Twig is pretty much the only person in seventh grade who wears a watch—and she only does it because her mom hates it. The face is a big plastic Hello Kitty, and her mom calls it "a travesty."

we're going to catch the 1:23 bus, we have to go now. And we have to run."

There was no time to change into better clothes, so I pulled my big wool coat over my cat-and-dog pajamas, and we tiptoed out of the house, careful not to make too much sound.

And then we were outside, in the cold night air, ready for this last, unexpected phase of Operation Egg. Snow whirled around us, murking everything into a white haze, and I shivered as chunks of wet ice landed on my face.

I breathed in the icy air, and I was ready to run when someone asked, "What's the plan?"

I blinked through the snowy haze, once, twice, and how did I not see him before? Dari, standing in front of us, fists shoved into his pockets, shoulders hunched up to his ears. He rocked back and forth on his heels with cold and discomfort.

"What?" I said, because that was the only thing I could say. My emotions were moving too quickly— I could hardly keep track. Hopelessness, confusion, excitement, and now a hot flame of anger. "What are you doing here?"

"Guys, we have to get to the bus stop," Twig said, her words rushing together. She looked at me, eyes pleading.

Dari opened his mouth to say something, but we were already late, and I took off running. I slipped and slid in the snow, but I kept my footing because to fall now would be to fail. My footsteps and heartbeat sounded like *orchid, orchid, orchid.*

Twig being here felt right, but Dari threw everything off. I didn't know him well enough, not yet, and he wasn't my best friend. Everything Twig had said about the two of us felt empty now.

Even though the logical side of me knew it was probably unfair, I wanted to scream at Twig for bringing Dari, for telling him about the orchid. That was something Mikayla might have done—but not Twig. If we hadn't been sprinting for the bus, I would have shouted horrible things. I would have said never mind about Operation Orchid and also maybe never mind about our friendship, because how could she tell him about this? How could she bring him into the secrets and adventures that were supposed to be ours?

We showed up at the bus stop at 1:23 a.m. exactly. The bus wasn't there. Two minutes later, still no sign of it.

"No, no," Twig said, once she'd stopped panting. "I think we missed it!" That did not make me less angry with her. "We missed it!" she said again, because Twig has no idea when to stop.

"Natalie," Dari said cautiously, because unlike her, he has some sense and could tell I was upset. "Twig told me about your flower."

No duh, Dari.

"I know I let you down with the egg drop. I made those tweaks and . . . it was my fault we lost. But I want to make it up to you. Whatever the plan is, I want you to know I'm here. I'm in." Then he got all awkward and mumbly and added, "Because we're a team."

Just as he said that, the bus turned the corner and pulled up to the stop, so I was saved from having to respond. I still don't know what I would have said. *I'm glad you're here, Dari* or *Go home, Dari* or *How much did Twig tell you, Dari?* Because I wanted to say all of those things, but all of them were slightly wrong, too.

In the end I didn't say anything. Twig pulled bus fare for all of us out of her pocket, and the bus driver didn't bat an eye.

Twig hesitated, and for the first time that night— maybe even the first time ever—I saw uncertainty in her eyes. I think both of us half expected to be stopped right there. We were so used to being stopped by adults that I think we expected the driver to stand up, put his hands on his hips, and say, *Excuse me, young children, but isn't it a little late to be out on your own?* And then he'd drive us back home and *oh well,* at least we'd tried.

"Well," the driver said, smacking bright green chewing gum against his front teeth, "are you getting on or not?" He was tall and skinny, skinnier than Dari even, in a way that looked like his bones might rip right through his skin with one wrong move.

We got on. Of course we got on. We were following the procedure.

The only other person on the bus was a homeless man, sitting near the front and drinking out of a paper-bagged bottle, so we sat down in the very back of the bus.

Twig whispered to me, "What kind of bus driver lets three seventh graders onto a bus in the middle of the night by themselves?" But I didn't answer, because I was still mad at her, and also because I don't believe in questioning good luck.

Twig leaned over and filled Dari in on the procedure, and then we fell silent. The landscape changed around us, and the bus groaned as it made its way out of my neighborhood, into streets full of broken buildings.

The homeless man started laughing and laughing, at nothing and nobody. My palms got all sweaty and my heart beat fast, and I told myself I was just excited. This feeling: just excitement.

I'd ridden the bus to the Lancaster University lab once before, years ago when Mom's car wouldn't start and she still needed to get to work. I had sighed and jittered my knees up down up down up down so our seats shook, because I hated being on the bus. I liked driving with Mom or Dad in the tiny, private space of our car, and the bus felt wide and open and crawling with other people's lives.

But Mom had placed one hand on my shaking knee and said, "This is our adventure, Natalie." She pointed to the woman in the front of the bus, cradling a baby against her chest, and made up a story: "That's her first child, and she named the baby Violet, because violets bloom in May." Just like that, the big bus cramped full of other people's lives hadn't seemed so bad anymore.

Now the bus driver braked quickly for a red light, and liquid sloshed out of the homeless man's paper-bagged bottle and onto the floor. He swore loudly, and his mouth sounded filled with marbles.

I hadn't even realized my legs were shaking. I gripped my knees until they stopped.

"How much longer?" Twig whispered, and I couldn't tell if she was asking out of excitement or impatience or fear. For the first time, I realized I couldn't read her. Tonight was a night of firsts for Twig, I guess. Or maybe this was just the first time I was noticing.

"Five more stops," Dari said. He was fiddling with something small and pink, rubbing it back and forth in his hand. "Just five more stops. Count them, Twig." I realized then that it was the tiny flamingo. Twig had decided to give it to him after all.

Twig relaxed beside me, so I guess she had been

nervous, too. I hated that I hadn't been the one to make her feel better.

We rolled past another stop, where nobody got on, because nobody else in the world was awake right now except for the three of us, the bus driver, and the homeless man. Twig reached out and squeezed my hand so tight, and I squeezed back, and we counted the stops— five, four, three, two, one. I reached up and tugged the yellow cord, and the bus hadn't even stopped before we were running to the front, lurching and swaying with that giant hunk of metal.

"Ain't it a little late for three little bits?" the man said, pointing his bottle at us in accusation, but I clamped onto Twig's hand and pulled her off the bus before she could respond.

The bus driver didn't say anything at all, didn't even give us a glance before cranking the doors shut and roaring away. And then the street was silent, and the three of us stood on the sidewalk, hugging our arms against our chests.

"Well, I guess we should walk to the lab now," Dari said, his jaw clenched, his face pale.

I turned on my heel and started walking past the dorms and the academic buildings, toward Mom's lab. Two giggling college girls in miniskirts and Ugg boots walked past us, giving us sideways glances and then giggling even harder into their hands, but they didn't question us. We kept walking. I hadn't been here in months, but I knew the way—it was etched deep down in my bones. This was kind of like coming home. I reminded myself to be excited. I reminded myself that this was a good thing.

ASSIGNMENT 35: ALL THE FORGOTTEN THINGS

Back when Mom worked, she was in the lab constantly, especially in those last few months with the Cobalt Blue Orchid, sacrificing late nights, weekends, even holidays. Mom loved her job. But she loved me, too.

Instead of enrolling me in preschool, she'd taken me to the lab with her, and I'd never stopped tagging along. I even had my own white coat. I think it was from an old student intern, some short girl from Montana, but it became mine and I loved it. I never felt like I was very good at science, but I loved the lab. I loved being with Mom, away from my normal life filled with school and homework and, later, filled with Mikayla being all weird.

Mikayla stopped coming to the lab in fifth grade. She had Better Things to Do.

I'm not sure what I expected to feel when we walked up to that massive building, but I thought my heart would match the occasion. I shouldn't have been so afraid. I should have felt happy or excited or just *right,* because I was so close to fixing my family and putting everything back together, just the way it was supposed to be.

But late at night, the building loomed, looking not at all the way I remembered it.

"We can do this," Twig whispered into my ear, as if she could sense my fear. I was still a little upset with her, but her words helped. Twig was good like that.

I reached into my pocket and pulled out Mom's keys, holding them with shaking hands.

"Do you need some help?" Dari said as I fumbled with the lock. "The cold is making your fingers numb, so it's hard for you to grip the key. I have gloves, so—"

"I got it, Dari," I said. I knew he was trying to be helpful, but I couldn't stand him right then. Just looking at him made my blood bubble with that Not Right feeling, and I didn't want to hear his voice.

I got the first lock opened, and then moved on to the dead bolt. We stood outside in the cold, the winter air whipping through the thin cotton of my pajama pants. I think we froze to death and came back to life and then froze all over again before I finally got us inside.

The lobby of the building was clean and sleek and full of oddly shaped lamps. A guard sat slumped over the front desk, his snores echoing. I'd forgotten about the guard, somehow—guards had never been a problem when I was with Mom. She'd smile and wave and say hello, but this was a guard I'd never seen before. So much had changed, in just a few months.

Twig whispered, "This place looks like a fancy Ikea catalog," which was funny and true, but we didn't dare laugh. Dari raised his pointer finger to his lips and held it there as we tiptoed through the lobby, moving so slowly we hardly moved at all.

The elevator would have made too much noise, so we chose the stairs instead, pushing the door to the stairwell open, holding our breaths as we clicked it shut. The three of us climbed those steps, all the way to the lab on the third floor, and when Twig glanced over at me, with those wide, wild eyes, I knew exactly what she was thinking.

This time, we really were like secret agent spies. No more pretending.

When we made it to the third floor, we stood in front of big glass doors, in the tiny space between the stairs and elevator and the lab.

Twig looked at me. "Well, do you want to do the honors?"

So I did the honors. I pushed Mom's third key into the lock and opened the doors, and we were inside. It was all so familiar: the long hallway entrance, the offices lining the white walls, and the white tiled floors. I was excited and heartsick, all at once, and I almost didn't hear the quiet ticking underneath the sound of my own heartbeat, but Twig did.

"Natalie," she said. I followed Twig's gaze toward the tiny code box, which was flashing blue on the wall. *Click, click, click,* it went, all quiet like it didn't really want to bother you. Like it was saying, *Um, excuse me, but, uh, you're intruding?*

"Do you know the code?" Dari asked.

I didn't. This, too, I don't know how I'd forgotten. How many times had I gone to Mom's lab? How many times had I seen her punch the code in after entering? One last security measure, just in case—just in case three kids broke into the lab at 2:00 a.m.

I should've watched Mom more carefully. I should have paid attention. "Um," I said, because that's the only answer I could give.

"Natalie," Twig said again, panic blooming in her voice.

"Right," I said, moving toward the alarm box. The flashing blue looked like police lights, but at least it wasn't loud. At least I could think.

I typed 1111, but the light kept flashing.

"I don't think that's the code," Dari said.

I could have killed him, right there, but I didn't. I typed in 2222. The box kept flashing.

"Natalie!" Twig said.

I didn't have a plan. This wasn't in the procedure. I did the only thing I could think to do next. I typed 3333.

And then the flashing stopped.

"Three-three-three-three?" Dari said. "That's the code? Really?"

I started laughing, this wild kind of laugh that I couldn't control. Twig started laughing, too, and then we were both shouting, "Three-three-three-three! Three-three-three-three!"

Dari stood there, looking at us like the whole world had gone upside down. "How is that the code? Did you know it before?"

I laughed and shook my head. "I just guessed!" My voice belonged to a happy, carefree girl, and I almost didn't recognize it.

"But—" Dari said, shaking his head.

And Twig threw an arm around his shoulder and said, "Sometimes good things just happen. Sometimes you get lucky."

Finally, all that *dduk* luck had paid off. My mind was a chorus of *finally, finally, finally.*

Dari took a huge breath and shook his head, but a smile spread across his face. "All right," he said. "Let's get Natalie her flower."

ASSIGNMENT 36: OBSERVATIONS

The orchid wasn't hard to find. I went all the way to the far end of the lab, to Mrs. Menzer's side of the filing cabinet, where she'd pulled out the seed all those years ago. That moment was burned into my memory. I opened the drawer labeled GARDENING: MISC. and rummaged until I found a translucent blue ziplock bag like the one she'd pulled the seed from. Everything Mrs. Menzer did was color-coded.

My hands shook as I ripped open the bag and pulled out a seed. There were three left in there, but I only took one. I only needed one. I pinched the bag closed and placed it back in the drawer, and that's when I noticed the label: IRIS GERMANICA.

But that was a mistake. This wasn't an iris. This was my orchid. My *Cattleya fortis*.

Orchidaceae. *Cattleya*. *Fortis*.

I searched quickly around in the drawer, but there weren't any other bags.

"Is that what you came for?" Dari asked, and I could tell he was watching me and piecing all his observations together, trying to analyze the mystery of me, so I turned away and clutched the seed to my chest. Something was wrong that *couldn't* be wrong. This had to be right. I played back the memory I'd burned into my heart, but I knew this was where she'd pulled the seed from. Maybe the bag was labeled wrong.

"It's the orchid!" Twig yelped, practically tackling me into a hug.

Finding the seed should have been a celebration, but now I had all these questions. I felt as if I'd been working out a giant scientific mystery all this time, and I hadn't even known it, and now all my questions and observations and data were *click-click-click*ing. And all I wanted was to get straight home before everything snapped together.

"We have to go," I said, still grasping the little seed. My nails dug into the heel of my hand, but I didn't care. I didn't explain the urgency to my friends—I don't think I could have even explained it to myself—but I felt like I needed to get out, like I needed to get home and plant that seed right this very second, or else, or else—

I led them back through the winding lab halls, needing to get to that elevator, needing to get home, and we were almost to those big glass doors when I stopped. I stood right in front of Mom's office, and my feet wouldn't budge. I was squeezing the seed so hard that my right hand was going numb.

"Are you all right?" Twig asked. But I didn't answer. I just stared up at the name on the door. ALICE NAPOLI. My mother's name, my mother's office, even though she hadn't been to work in months. Even though she'd been fired.

The questions pounded in my head. When Dad got extra stressed at work, he'd pinch the bridge of his nose and say, *Migraine.* It all seemed so old and adult, but I was sure this was what a migraine felt like—having so many questions crowded in your brain, and not quite being able to touch the answers.

I ran through a list of observations in my head, a trail of clues:

- Mrs. Menzer had told Dad, "We miss her."
- Mom still had her office keys.
- Mom's name was still on her office door.

I could feel Twig getting restless behind me, could hear the *swish-swish* of her coat as she fidgeted, but then

Dari said, "Twig and I will wait by the glass doors. You take your time."

I could have hugged Dari, even if I didn't want him there. Sometimes you needed Dari and his way of understanding.

"Thanks, Dari," I said, and I felt all that anger whoosh out of me. It wasn't his fault Twig invited him, after all, and I knew he was just trying to be a good friend. Maybe he wasn't my best friend, but we were still a team.

I heard my friends leave, and the big glass doors shut, and then I turned the knob to Mom's office all the way before stepping inside. *Quick, quiet.*

Her office was the same as it had always been.

There was the couch where I used to nap, read, do homework. There was the checkered rug where Mikayla and I did our experiments, the purple stain where we'd mixed baking soda and vinegar—and a whole bottle of bubble bath. And there was Mom's desk and her pictures of Dad and me, and her calendar that was stuck in July. Why was this office still hers, still exactly the same, if she'd been fired?

I didn't realize I'd been moving through the office until I was picking up those framed photos, those happy, smiley, million-years-ago pictures of our perfect family. I gripped the family photo of us at Disneyland so hard that the edge of the glass frame pressed into my hand and I wished I could escape into the memory.[54]

"Natalie, Natalie!" Twig's voice came from the hallway, followed by the sound of slamming doors and loud footsteps.

Twig ran into Mom's office, her hair flying around her face, as if every strand were fleeing in panic. *"Natalie!"* she said again, breathless.

Behind her, a security guard appeared, with Dari trailing behind him, and the guard stood right there in Mom's doorway.

I dropped the frame. And it shattered at my feet.

---

[54] Dad, Mom, and me, wearing our Mickey ears in front of Fantasyland, that trip where Mom scheduled our whole vacation down to the minute, and we didn't mind one bit.

ASSIGNMENT 37: CRIMINALS

My panic filled the whole room, and the guard filled the whole doorway. He was big and tall, with thick black glasses and a name tag that read JOE. To be honest, that was a bit of a relief, because Joe is a friendly-sounding name.

He stared at us as we stared at him, and we were all frozen in one moment. Then he tugged at his right earlobe and said, "Um?"

I guess he hadn't expected to see three kids breaking into a botany lab.

"Uh," I said.

"Good morning," Twig said.

Dari stood behind Joe, gripping his hair with one hand, face pale with horror.

"You triggered the alarm system," Joe said, shaking his head like he wasn't sure why he was explaining himself. "If you type in the wrong code three times, I get an alert."

"So three-three-three-three *wasn't* the right code!" Dari said, and then snapped his mouth shut like he hadn't meant to speak.

So I guess I hadn't been that lucky. All that *dduk* for nothing.

Joe frowned. "I should maybe call the police?" he said, as if it were a question.

"No," Dari gasped. I'd never seen him so unraveled, and I hated myself for letting him come. He had risked so much to be here, and he'd be in so much trouble. I didn't deserve a friend like that.

"Don't." I hesitated, but I knew what I had to do. I stepped forward, broken glass crunching beneath my sneakers. "Call Dana Menzer instead. She's the head of this lab. We're—we're friends of her daughter."

Twig made a choking noise.

Joe looked relieved to have an out, and he nodded, grabbing the cell phone clipped to his waist. "Uh." He looked at us like he had no idea what to do. I didn't blame him. This probably didn't happen too often. "Don't move."

He stepped outside to call Mikayla's mom, and Dari slipped inside the office. The three of us stood together, not saying a word, and then the guard came back in.

"She's coming." Joe sighed and sat in Mom's chair, gesturing to her couch. "It'll be a while." His voice was a shrug. We glanced at each other, debating, because kids in Big Trouble don't normally hang out on the couch, but we sat, because he was right. It probably would be a while.

And it was. For forty-five minutes nobody said anything. That was the worst forty-five minutes of our lives, sitting in silence and regret. My mind felt broken, stuck in an endless loop, and I couldn't think anything except: Mom *decided* to stop working. She stopped caring. And she stopped caring about me.

I'd be in trouble. Dari and Twig would be in trouble, too, and it was all my fault—all because I wanted to get up and fix everything, because I wanted to take charge and be the team captain and save my family.

What a ridiculous idea.

"I'm sorry," I said without looking up at my friends.

They didn't respond at first, and I thought, *They hate me, they hate me, they hate me.*

But then Dari whispered, "We're a team." And Twig made that soothing egg-cracking motion down my back, and my chest tightened.

Before I had a chance to respond, Mrs. Menzer arrived,

her footsteps thudding down the hallway, stopping at the door of Mom's office.

Joe jumped up in relief. "Do you need any help?"

Mrs. Menzer looked at the three of us and then at him, and then back at us. Her mouth opened and closed a couple times. With her curly hair gathered into a messy bun, and her sweatpants tucked into her boots, she looked like she'd rolled out of bed and stumbled into a bad dream.

I used to love Mikayla's mom. I used to think she was the second-best mom in the entire world, until she fired my mom and I decided to hate her. Only, she didn't really fire my mom, I guess. If I analyzed all those observations, all that data, that was the cold, hard truth. Mom stopped going to work because she didn't want to go anymore, or maybe because she couldn't.

And Mrs. Menzer had kept Mom's office the way it was—waiting, waiting for Mom to come back, just like we were. I wasn't sure how to feel anymore. My emotions spun around and around like a broken compass, not quite sure where to land.

Mrs. Menzer shook her head no, and the guard got out of there real quick.

Once we heard the glass doors slam shut and the elevator *ding-ding*ing down, she said, "What are you *doing* here?"

Twig said, "We got lost," which was probably the worst

lie she's ever come up with, and Twig has come up with some pretty bad lies under pressure.[55]

Mrs. Menzer frowned, but she looked more curious than angry. She was a scientist, after all. She kept her eyes on me and waited.

"Here's the truth," I said, and then I told the whole story, for the first time ever, spoken aloud so I could never get it back. And I was okay with that.

I told her about how Mom and I had planted the orchid she gave us. About how it grew and bloomed and how we loved it. About how I know the plant is a miracle. And then I told her the harder stuff, about how Mom stopped working and I thought she'd been fired, but really she'd just stopped. About how the plant died—how we'd killed a plant that could survive toxins and death. About New Mexico and losing the egg competition and how I needed to find another Cobalt Blue Orchid. How breaking into the lab had seemed like the last shred of hope.

"Because the flower is *magic,*" I said, my voice cracking. "And I need the magic to save her."

Dari's mouth hung in a little O, because whatever Twig had told him to get him here, it hadn't been the full story.

Mrs. Menzer's expression softened. "Oh, Natalie, I'm

---

[55] Once, Twig tried to crash some poor kid's birthday bowling party by saying we were Russian orphans. We tried to speak with Russian accents. We got kicked out.

sorry. That flower—it wasn't magic. It was just an interesting, unexpected anomaly."

I wanted to tell her I knew that, that I wasn't silly enough to think it was *actually* magic, but I got stuck on the way she said *was*. It *was* interesting.

"And you didn't kill a Cobalt Blue Orchid, sweetie." Mrs. Menzer bit her bottom lip. "I'm sorry, Natalie, but you should talk to your mom about the flower you grew."

And then I knew there was more to this terrible puzzle. Everything I'd thought about Mom had been a lie. She'd been wrong about the cereal egg—it broke. She'd given up on her work because it had gotten hard and she didn't want to keep going. She hadn't been fierce or bold or brave. She'd given up on me. "What *about* the flower we grew? What do you mean?" I asked. I didn't want to know. But I did.

Mrs. Menzer gave me a sad smile. "I'm going to call all your parents now. You three need to get home."

"What about the flower?" I asked again, because my world was shattering, and I needed the truth to build it back up.

But she shook her head and said, "You have to talk to your mother, Natalie." And then she turned to Twig and Dari and asked for their parents' phone numbers, and I knew the conversation was over. I wouldn't get any more answers. Not from her.

When Mrs. Menzer went outside to call our families, we stayed in our little huddle for a long time, and Twig said in this small voice, just like Dari's after the egg drop, "Will we still be friends after this?" Like, somehow that had become the depressing catchphrase of our friendship.

I wasn't the one who answered. Dari was. He said yes immediately, as if that never should have been a question in the first place, and that was when I knew I wanted them in my life forever. I'd do anything for them. Just as they had for me.

I tried to think of the right words to say, but I knew if I tried to speak now I would cry, and Dari saw the look on my face and nodded. Because that's the thing about best friends: they just get you.

Mrs. Menzer returned, and when she herded us out of the lab and into her shiny black BMW downstairs, we marched like inmates. After Twig and Dari got in, right as I was about to slide into the backseat, she tilted my chin up to her face and kissed my forehead.

I'd seen her do that to Mikayla so many times. Now she was giving some of that love to me, and I swallowed hard.

We drove back to the suburbs, through those streets full of broken buildings, and Mrs. Menzer dropped Dari off first, because his house was the closest.

"Thank you," I whispered into his ear as he got out of

the car. His lips were pressed into a thin line, anticipating his parents' anger, but he looked at me and nodded in a way that said, *Of course.*

"Good luck," Twig said, and then threw her arms around him. Dari couldn't seem to let her go.

"Come on now," Mrs. Menzer said in her gentle way, and she led Dari up to his house while Twig and I waited.

"I'm sorry," Twig said into the ringing silence of the empty car. "I shouldn't have called you about going to New Mexico. I should've just let things be."

"Me too," I said. "I shouldn't have dragged you into this."

"You didn't drag me into anything," she said fiercely. "I'm always going to be with you."

"But I was a terrible team captain," I blurted. "Everything we tried to do failed, and I got you guys in trouble."

"Natalie," Twig said, "you aren't the captain because you do everything right and stay out of trouble. You're the captain because you bring us all together."

I chewed my lip, not sure what to say. Part of me had always thought they'd be better off without me.

Then, more softly, she said: "I know I shouldn't have brought Dari. I knew you'd be upset. But I was scared, and he always knows the answers, and . . . I don't know."

I reached over and grabbed her hand. "It's okay. He does know a lot of answers." The truth is, I was glad she brought him. I was glad to have my friends.

And some things are better left unsaid, but then again, other things aren't. I looked over, right in her eyes, and she looked back. She seemed to glow in the light of the streetlamps. "I don't know what I would do without you guys," I told her. "Especially *you*, Twig."

She unbuckled her seat belt and scooted over until she was pressed right up next to me, and she laid her head on my shoulder. "Me neither."

After a long while, Mrs. Menzer came back to the car. She swallowed hard, but she didn't say anything about her conversation with Dari's parents. Twig and I peeked through the window, but Dari's front door was already shut. The lights to his house were on, but we couldn't see anything.

"Do you think he'll be all right?" I asked.

Twig swallowed. "I don't know."

Twig was next, and I waited in the car again while Mrs. Menzer walked her up to her front porch. Alone, I expected to feel guilty and sad and scared, but I didn't feel any of those things. I felt okay. Twig's mom opened the door right away and dropped to her knees, hugging Twig. No matter how strange her mom acted, I could see she loved her daughter. She would always love her daughter.

When Mrs. Menzer walked back to the car, she looked like she might cry. I didn't know why, but adults are strange, and maybe the night was just sad for everyone. "Thank you, Mrs. Menzer," I said when she got in.

She turned around to look at me in the backseat. "You're all so young," she said.

I didn't know how to respond, because it's always so awkward when adults comment on your age. They look at you and say *You're still so young* or *You're getting so old,* and you want to shake your head and say *I'm not young or old. I'm just me.*

"Mikayla always tells me how funny you and Twig are," she said. And it took all my willpower not to be like, *Wait, what?* And then she added, "I think she misses you."

I had to put the whole conversation out of my head because adults have no idea what they're talking about—and if I'd thought about that any more, my brain might have exploded. This night was already too much, and I think Mrs. Menzer sensed that because she didn't say anything else on the drive to my house.

We were home before I could prepare myself, because Twig's house is close to mine, and because maybe I never would have been ready.

"Ready?" Mrs. Menzer asked.

I wanted to laugh or cry—I wasn't sure. We walked up to my front door, and my parents flung it open before we rang the doorbell. Mom knelt and wrapped me into her, and she smelled like a strange mix of old and new—like her flower shampoo and a newer, deeper scent of dark chocolate. Part of me wanted to pull away, and part of me couldn't let go.

I could feel Mom look up at Mrs. Menzer over my shoulder, and I don't know what they were communicating in their silent way, and for once I didn't want to investigate. I didn't need all the answers. Not tonight, anyway.

Dad talked to Mrs. Menzer for a few minutes, making a lot of *mhmmm* and *mmmm* sounds, already in Therapist Mode. But I didn't listen to their conversation. I just let myself be held. I let Mom hold me.

I tried to freeze time.

But Mrs. Menzer finally left, and Mom pulled away first, holding me by the shoulders and leaving a gaping empty space between us. "Natalie," she said. "What happened?"

She sounded tired. I *was* tired.

I ripped out of her hands, stepping back. "I had to!" I said, vaguely aware that I was screaming. "I had to go because you couldn't go. I had to. But this whole time, you didn't care and you didn't tell me anything. You told me she fired you!" I said, even though, thinking about it, I knew that wasn't true. I had just assumed.

"Natalie, Natalie, Natalie," Dad was saying. He knelt, too, so I stood in front of them, slightly taller than both my parents.

I wanted to shove them. I wanted to collapse.

"You gave up on me!"

"Natalie, please," Mom said, reaching for my hand, but I pulled away again. She had tears in her eyes.

I did, too, and the whole world went blurry. "I just . . . ," I began, trying to make sense of the jumbled thoughts in my brain, but I couldn't continue. I couldn't form words.

Dad put one hand on Mom's shoulder and one hand on mine. "I think it might be best if we all got some sleep tonight. We can talk about this tomorrow."

I closed my eyes and nodded, grateful because I couldn't possibly talk anymore. I couldn't possibly *feel* anymore.

He and Mom stood, and they walked me to my bedroom. Dad hugged me. "Get some sleep, Natalie. We love you."

My parents exchanged one of those looks I couldn't understand, and he went back to bed while Mom stayed by my bed, stroking my hair as sleep reached up and sucked me under.

ASSIGNMENT 38:
A WORD ON WORDS

When I came downstairs this morning, Mom and Dad were already sitting on the couch, all dressed and waiting for me. I was nervous after the scene I'd caused, and I knew I was about to get hard-core Therapisted.

I sat down in the chair across from them, but Dad shook his head. "Sit with us, Nats," he said, so I moved over to the couch and sat right between them. Mom started stroking my hair again, but she didn't say anything. Dad was leading the show now, like he had been since summer.

"What were you thinking?" he asked, trying to keep his voice steady and level, trying to keep the exasperation and fear and frustration out. Trying, and failing.

I couldn't say anything. I didn't want to explode like I had last night. I bit my lip and curled my knees into my chest and stared at my toes. Mom wrapped her arm around my shoulders and squeezed me into her, just as Dad said, "Natalie, why did you go there?"

I felt myself curling in, into my sleeping-grass silence, but it was time to stop holding back. "The Cobalt Blue Orchid died, and I had to get another one." It sounded so simple, but there it was.

"But, Natalie, the orchid . . . ," Mom began, and then: understanding.

Horror pierced Mom's face, the first true emotion to shatter her wall of pleasant, half-true smiles and utter, utter blankness. The first emotion, and it was horror, and that was all my fault.

"Oh, Natalie," Mom said. She looked lost, and Dad kept quiet.

I saw him struggle to keep quiet, and I knew he was letting the silence build, but I started talking before the silence could take over. I wouldn't be tricked into talking—I didn't need to be. Because I was done with the secrets and the quiet and the walking on eggshells. This time I chose to speak.

I turned to Mom. "You said the orchid is magic. And you loved it. You *loved* it. And then it was dead, and I thought maybe if I could replace it, we could start all over. We could have another chance and it would be like none of this ever happened. I wanted to win the egg drop money to go to New Mexico, but we lost, and Twig was saying let's fly to New Mexico, but we knew we couldn't, so we went to the lab instead—"

"Natalie—" Mom said again, but I wasn't ready to stop. I was finally getting my thoughts in order. I was finally telling the truth.

"I thought maybe that's why you were so sad, because your miracle flower—because you couldn't do your research anymore and you loved that research more than anything. But our orchid died and that was the last one you had and you couldn't go back to the lab. . . ." I didn't finish that last part, because I guess it wasn't true. She *could* have gone back.

Mom was shaking her head and she wore the exact same expression that Mikayla's mom had last night, and I wanted to shout, *Don't say it!* But I bit my lip and let her speak. "That flower in our greenhouse, Natalie, it wasn't an orchid. Mrs. Menzer gave you a Blue Bearded Iris."

I didn't understand. I wanted to tell her she was confused and wasn't making sense, because of course our plant was a Cobalt Blue Orchid.

"We had a very limited amount of the Cobalt Blue Orchids, Nats, and they're very delicate—we had to keep all of them in the lab. We couldn't have given any away."

She seemed desperate to make me understand, but I didn't.

"Mrs. Menzer was feeling bad about your friendship with Mikayla, and she thought it might help if you had your own project. I guess the Blue Bearded Iris looks similar to the Cobalt Blue Orchid, but I didn't realize . . ." She shook her head slowly, her eyes fixed on a different time, a different life. "I probably should've known you'd think that. We'd been talking about the orchid just a few days before."

I should've known the difference between an iris and an orchid—they weren't *that* similar—but I'd been too caught up in the magic.

Mom kept talking. This was the most I'd heard her talk in months, as if all of a sudden she remembered how. "We were doing research on the Cobalt Blue Orchid because we thought its ability to process those chemicals might have some big implications for diseases. If we got lucky. But we didn't.

"We weren't able to isolate those properties or graft them onto other plants. The funding fell through. Dana had to make a tough call as the department head when she decided to shut down the project. It wasn't easy for either of us."

Mom took a big breath. Silent tears spilled from her eyes, and she looked at Dad with such desperation, like she wanted him to save her. And Dad, he looked right back, and I could see the desperation in his eyes, because he wanted to save her, too, but he didn't know how.

"Natalie," she said, and then she looked at me--really looked at me. "I should have talked to you about all this. We should have been talking."

I shook my head and buried myself into my knees, because I couldn't stand to see the apologies written in my parents' eyes. I hurt for all of us, even for that little dead iris that was never as special as I wanted it to be.

"I love you, Natalie," Mom said into my ear. "I've been—I've been depressed, but that doesn't mean I don't love you, always. I am *so* sorry." Her voice shook, as if the words were heavy, impossible to lift out of her, but she did it anyway, because she loved us.

"We will get through this," Dad said. His voice was rough and strong, and even if he was broken, he would put himself back together. For us, he would pick up all the little pieces.

"I'm so sorry, my Natalie," Mom said again.

And that was when I started crying. I cracked open and cried like I would never stop crying, like I would cry until all of me was gone. I was too afraid to look up from my curled-up cocoon and see my parents, because they weren't the Mom and Dad I used to know. They were so much more now. Not perfect, not magic—but real.

I was a different Natalie, too, and I'm not sure how we're supposed to fit together as a family anymore.

I cried until somehow, impossibly, I had no tears left, and they held me and didn't let go. They didn't leave, and we kept moving, swinging forward. One breath at a time.

ASSIGNMENT 39: SUPERVISED PHONE CALLS

Twig called today after school. "I'm only able to call because my mom is at work and Hélène took pity on me." Our cell phones were confiscated, on account of the whole sneaking-out-and-breaking-and-entering thing.

"I'm only able to talk because my dad is standing right next to me," I said. Dad gave a sad smile from across the table. Mom was actually seeing a therapist this afternoon,[56] so it was just Dad and me, and he wasn't about to let me out of his sight. Trust was an issue now, and I couldn't exactly blame him.

---

[56] Not Doris, though. Guiltily, I had kind of been relieved about that. I've come to like her, believe it or not, and I want her to be just mine.

"Are you grounded?" Twig asked.

"More or less," I said, because I wasn't quite sure. I was supposed to come home after school every day, and we were going to spend more Family Time together, but somehow that didn't seem like a punishment. "You?"

"Same," said Twig. "My mom isn't too thrilled about our grand adventure. But we'll still see each other at school." We'd seen each other today, but it hadn't felt like enough. We'd had to act like everything was fine, especially around Mikayla, who kept shooting us looks that we tried to ignore.

"We'll still be friends after this," I said.

Twig laughed. I loved Twig for that, for her infectious happiness. "Duh."

"Have you talked to Dari?" I asked. He hadn't been in school today.

She hesitated. "No. I called, but nobody picked up."

"Hopefully he'll be in class tomorrow."

"Yeah. I'm worried about him." Twig's voice broke, and I realized she was different from the Twig I had always known. I wondered if Twig had changed last night or sometime long before that. Perhaps she'd been this new Twig for a long time, and I just hadn't noticed.

"I better go. Hélène's giving me a look. I just wanted to see how you were."

"I'm okay," I said.

"I'll see you tomorrow."

"Yeah. Love you, Twig."

She laughed. "I love you, too, you freak of nature."

We had changed and would continue to change, but Twig would always be my best friend.

When we hung up, Dad grimaced and shook his head. "The three of you really shouldn't have snuck out."

"I know."

And then Dad made like he was going to say something else but decided not to.

"What is it?" I asked, because I wanted him to speak. I wanted him to always speak, no matter what.

"But since you did," he sighed, "I'm glad the three of you were together. I'm glad none of you were alone."

I looked down at my hands, but Dad kept talking. "You have good friends, Natalie." I couldn't look at him, because he was right—I did—so maybe I did get lucky after all.

Dad got up from his seat and walked over to me. He knelt by my chair and held my hands in his. "And you have your mom and me, too. I know we haven't been perfect, but we will always love you. No matter what happens, Natalie, you will never, ever be alone."

I kept my eyes on our hands. He had long, thin fingers, like my grandmother. "Dad?" I forced myself to speak. I already knew—but I still needed to *hear* the truth, spoken aloud. "Mom was sick like this before. She was depressed before." I'd meant to ask it as a question, but it didn't come out that way.

Dad squeezed my hands. "When you were very young. The two of you stayed in bed together for a month."

I had already known, but now I *knew*. This terrible, incomprehensible thing that had descended upon our lives wasn't new at all. It had always been there. I just hadn't understood it. I wasn't even sure I completely understood now, but I was doing my best.

"This situation—this depression—isn't her fault. She's trying, Natalie," he said.

"I know."

"I'm trying, too." Dad sounded like he was pleading his case. "I wanted to get her help earlier. I really did."

He looked at me like I was going to be angry. And I was, but I surprised myself by feeling hopeful, too. "I know," I said, and I squeezed his hands right back.

ASSIGNMENT 40: THE GREENHOUSE

I found Mom in the greenhouse, where the windows fogged from the warmth inside. Entering felt like walking into a different reality.

Mom looked real again, with her long strawberry-blond hair clipped back and her hands coated with dirt. "The little plant was dying," she said. "I found it in a pot in the corner."

She tucked my little Korean Fire plant into the soil, and so I told her about its name and its story and about how it blooms, always, even in the winter.

"It was your Christmas present," I said. She already knew that last part—it had been wrapped with a bow and a card—but I still wanted her to hear it. I was still angry with her.

She was quiet for a long time, patting the soil, even though the flower was already planted. But her voice was strong and clear when she said, "I love it."

She looked like Mom again, with her Serious Business hair and her dirty hands and her crackling eyes, but she wasn't exactly the same. I hadn't really known the sad version of her, but I didn't know this version, either. The version of her that was everything put together— hope and hopelessness, curiosity and courage, failure and fight. She wasn't perfect. She didn't know everything. But she was still my mom, still here. And I still loved her.

"I planted the iris seed," she said, gesturing to the empty spot where the old iris once lived. The iris that was nothing special, nothing magical or important, just a plain old nothing iris.

"Why?" I said. I wish I could've kept the anger out of my voice, but I had buried everything deep for so long, and now all of it was bursting through the surface.

Mom always planted seeds, anywhere and everywhere. If there wasn't room in the greenhouse, she'd find a tiny patch, and if there *really* wasn't room, she'd find a space on the side of the road. Whenever I'd ask her about it, she'd shrug and say, "Plants are beautiful."

And so when I asked why, I expected her usual answer: beauty for beauty's sake. But instead she looked right at me, eyes full of hope and the shimmery hint of tears, and said, "Because we deserve a second chance."

ASSIGNMENT 41: THE SCIENCE OF BREAKABLE THINGS

Mr. Neely had us present our scientific process projects this week. Twig, Dari, and I would be giving a joint presentation about the egg drop, and since Twig was in charge of bringing our poster board presentation, she was getting a ride with her mom that morning. I biked to school alone and was locking up my bike just as Mikayla got out of her car. I guess that's what Mom and Dad would call coincidence, but I kind of think it was fate.

There were two sides of me, right then, the old Natalie, who would have tucked her head down and walked into the classroom, and the new Natalie, who walked right up to the car. I kept my head up and my feet moving forward.

"Hi," I said once I reached the car.

Mikayla was pulling a cardboard tray full of potted plants out of the backseat, and she looked at me with an expression that was not quite surprise.

Mikayla's mom rolled the passenger window down and said, "Hello, Natalie."

"Hi," I said again, because sometimes, after someone has seen the truest parts of you, little words are enough. "Do you need help?" I asked Mikayla, not because I really wanted to help, but because I felt like I should offer.

"I got it," she said as she readjusted the tray and slammed the car door shut with her thigh. I was kind of glad she said no. It's not like we were about to skip into school, carrying the plants and singing songs.

"Have a nice day," Mrs. Menzer said, and her smile was kind and knowing, and I didn't turn away. I smiled back.

When she drove off, Mikayla and I walked into the school and started up the steps to the third floor. I hooked my thumbs into my backpack straps, just to have something to do with my hands. And the old me wouldn't have said anything, but this whole say-what-you're-feeling thing? It's pretty nice. "I'm not really sure why you stopped being my friend," I said.

Mikayla looked over at me, and for a second, her face opened up. Her eyebrows rose and her lips parted, like

281

she was so surprised by what I'd said that she didn't have time to roll her eyes or sneer. "*I* didn't stop being *your* friend."

I stared at her, trying to come up with a good response. But what are you supposed to say when you find out someone's living in a totally different universe?

"You became best friends with Twig, and I couldn't compete with that. Like, the second you saw her, you thought she was so shiny and awesome and whatever, so what was I supposed to do?" Then she did roll her eyes, just for good measure. "And anyway, you guys are too weird for me."

"Mikayla," I said, but I couldn't really comprehend what she was saying. I'd spent so much time worrying about how much Mikayla had hurt me that I'd never really stopped to think about how I'd hurt her. "I'm sorry. I didn't mean—"

But Mikayla rolled her eyes again. "It's whatever, Natalie. I don't care anymore. And I know what happened, by the way. With you guys breaking into the lab—which is seriously stupid."

I opened my mouth to speak, to ask her to keep it a secret, but she looked at me and sighed. "Don't worry. I'm not going to tell anybody. I haven't told anybody yet, have I?"

Four years ago, Mikayla and I picked plants and created make-believe cures, and we didn't have a wisp of weirdness between us. Four years ago, we were different people.

"Thanks," I said.

A smile tugged at her lips, even if she tried to hide it. "You're literally not even interesting enough to gossip about."

We got to our lockers, and I helped her slide the cardboard tray into hers. She didn't say thank you, but she didn't need to. We could never go back to being best friends, but maybe things didn't have to be so bad between us anymore. Maybe things could be okay.

I went to sit with Dari in front of his locker as he put the finishing touches on our presentation. Dari was still grounded, pretty much indefinitely. Although that didn't seem to change his life so much. He was still doing homework, always.

He sat hunched over our poster board, checking it for the millionth time. He'd written all the facts and numbers in the center of the board, but he'd also painted a border of smiling eggs to add an "artistic design element." He'd used a drawing compass to outline them, so they looked more like happy polka dots than like eggs—but they were perfect if you asked me.

Twig got to school just before the second bell. She burst up from the stairwell, waving her crumpled presentation notes over her head, and when she saw Dari's egg border, she squealed and tackle-hugged him.

Things had worked out all right.

Later, in science class, we presented first, because Dari wanted to, and I guess we kinda owed him that much. We all talked about S'meggs, then Twig talked about velocity and Dari talked about angles.

And when it was finally my turn to present my question and research, I said, "I've been wondering about breakable things, and how to protect them."

I looked over at Mr. Neely, and he grinned because it wasn't the most scientific question ever, but it was the right one.

And for our final assignment, we had to choose someone else's presentation to reflect on. As soon as Mr. Neely said it, a part of me knew whose project I would pick, but I still surprised myself by getting out my notebook when Mikayla did her presentation.

OBSERVATIONS:
- Mikayla Menzer has potted plants.
- She explains that one plant was a control, which grew in direct sunlight. The second and third plants grew in boxes, one with holes poked on the left side, the other with holes on the right.

- The second and third plants are bent all funny, toward the holes, and the third one even stretched its way through the holes, escaping from the darkness and reaching into the light.
- Mr. Neely says Mikayla did *#great!* but adds that she could have used a control plant that grew in the dark, without any light.
- Mikayla Menzer says he's right—that she didn't think of it. But I know she did. She just couldn't bear the thought of killing something.
- Mikayla Menzer tugs at her braid and says she's done.
- Mikayla Menzer still smells like sunscreen.

STEP 8:
ANALYZE YOUR RESULTS

What can you learn from your results? What would you do differently? Your journey has finally come to an end, and I hope you had as much fun as I did exploring, investigating, and experimenting! Turn in your lab notebooks on Friday, and have a great summer!

#TheEnd

MAY 30

ASSIGNMENT 42: ANALYZING, OR SOMETHING

I've been thinking more about perennial plants. About how sometimes life needs to go underground, bury itself deep to survive, and how maybe that's not a bad thing. It's just necessary. And that's okay.

And now all of those plants are blooming again, and they're reaching up to the sun, and suddenly the school year is over.

We have to turn in our lab notebooks now, and I considered saying I'd lost mine, because how can I turn this in when I was supposed to observe the world scientifically, objectively, and I so clearly haven't?

When it comes down to it, though, Mr. Neely asked us

to find something that intrigued us and study it with all our hearts. So here's my observations, Mr. Neely. Here's all my heart.

Last year, when our English teacher handed out composition notebooks and told us to write our deepest feelings, nobody took her seriously. How silly, we thought, to write our secrets where anybody could read them.

And yet somehow this Wonderings journal turned into the most important assignment I've ever had. I told Doris about it, in one of our sessions, and she was overjoyed in that dorky way of therapists. "It's so wonderful that you've found an outlet," she said, "a way to express yourself."

But somehow, after that day in the greenhouse with Mom, I pretty much stopped writing. I couldn't tell Doris that, of course, not after she'd gotten so excited, but the truth was, all of a sudden, I didn't need it anymore.

Because now I can speak.

Mom and Dad and I are being honest with each other. And, honestly, Mom is not completely back to the way she was, but she's going to therapy twice a week, and she even started working again, part-time. There's a whole lot of strength in that, and I feel proud knowing I'm her daughter.

The weird thing? That Blue Bearded Iris never grew. Mom and I waited for it to grow while the Korean Fire, our survivor flower, blossomed around it—but that iris seed refused to sprout.

"I think it's time to give up," I said as Mom and I worked in the garden, weeding and watering. It had been over a month since we planted the iris, and we still didn't speak much. There were still hard days and bad days, but we were in the greenhouse every day, side by side, even when there wasn't much work to be done. This was how we said we're trying.

Mom sighed. "We don't give up, Natalie." She ran her hand over that empty patch of dirt and said, "We keep going and try something new."

So Mom and I went to the plant nursery. We bought all the iris seeds they had, in every color, and then we bought some orchids, too.

Those flowers didn't take long to grow. They seemed to sprout overnight, like magic or science or something in between, and they filled nearly every nook and cranny of the greenhouse, bursting with color, growing fierce and bold and brave.

First nothing, then everything.

We walked through the greenhouse aisles, running our hands along the petals, stopping only when we reached that one empty spot. Nothing would grow where the blue iris had died. And I'm sure there's some explanation, something scientific, but it felt like more than that.

Here was this vacant space that demanded to be remembered. And as Mom and I stood there, I curled into her, breathing in her dark chocolate smell.

Maybe one day we'll visit that mysterious blue field in New Mexico. We'll walk through all those unnaturally bright flowers and talk about everything that happened in these past few months—maybe even in the past few years. One day Mom will tell me the complicated, messy truth of herself, and I'll analyze those last few observations, and we will swing forward—into the us that is always changing, always growing.

But right then, in that greenhouse, full of life and light and second chances, we were okay. As it turns out, you can't always protect breakable things. Hearts and eggs will break, and everything changes, but you keep going anyway.

Because science is asking questions. And living is not being afraid of the answer.

AUTHOR'S NOTE

Depression is not a dirty word. Depression is one of the most common mental disorders in the United States and is nothing to be ashamed of. If you or someone you love is struggling with depression or another mental illness, know you are not alone. Know there are people who can help.

If you need to talk, please contact the National Alliance on Mental Illness (NAMI):

1-800-950-6264

Or visit the NAMI website for resources: nami.org

ACKNOWLEDGMENTS

Sarah Davies, superhero agent extraordinaire, thank you a thousand times for reading an early version and saying, *Go deeper.* Thank you a million times for saying, *I know you can.* Huge thanks also to the rest of the Greenhouse team, as well as the amazing Rights People.

Chelsea Eberly, thank you for reading this book over and over. For understanding these characters, sometimes better than I do. And, of course, thank you for championing Natalie's story.

A huge thank-you to the rest of the Random House team: Mallory Loehr, Michelle Nagler, Katrina Damkoehler, Stephanie Moss, Barbara Bakowski, Christine Ma, Kelly McGauley, Julie Conlon, Adrienne Waintraub, Lisa Nadel, Kristin Schulz, Jillian Vandall, Emily Bamford, Joe English, Emily Bruce, and more. I am a lucky author.

Mama Keller, my first and favorite editor, thank you for believing in me always, ever since I penned the Pinky Detective Stories. For reading countless drafts of countless stories, for teaching me how to be a better writer. But most of all, thank you for showing me how to be a better person.

Papa Keller, thank you for demonstrating the value of hard work and determination. You lead by the best example. And Sunhi: you are the Twig to my Natalie, a radiant source of humor and kindness and love, my sister and my best friend. Grandpa, thanks for letting me use your apartment as a temporary office (and for putting up with Spike).

Massive thanks to the friends who read drafts: Adelina, for supporting me back in high school when I whispered, *I'm writing a book;* Lila, for your love and honesty; Sam, for "fixing" books; Booki, for derp-ing through the industry with me. We've come a long way since our intern days. Thanks also to Tanaz for reading, and to the Swankys and Electrics.

Jabberwocks, thank you for your enthusiasm and support. Thank you for being my work family.

Lois Ann Yamanaka, Sandy Chang, Liz Foster, Alison Lazzara, and Dan Torday—thank you for word lists, prompts, assignments, and critiques. Thank you, too, for reminding me that I have something to say—and that's a good thing.

And of course Josh Nadel, my first reader: you are my rock. Thank you for reading drafts and washing dishes and saying "Cobalt Blue Orchid." This book wouldn't be the same without you, and neither would I.

ABOUT THE AUTHOR

TAE KELLER grew up in Honolulu, where she wrote stories, ate Spam musubi, and participated in her school's egg drop competition. (She did not win.) After graduating from Bryn Mawr College, she moved to New York City to work in publishing, and she now has a very stubborn Yorkie and a multitude of books as roommates. Visit her at TaeKeller.com, follow her on Twitter at @TaeKeller, and subscribe to her newsletter at bit.ly/taekellernews.